# Scorned QUEEN

NEW YORK TIMES BESTSELLING AUTHOR
# LISA RENEE JONES

Copyright © 2024 Julie Patra Publishing/Lisa Renee Jones

All rights reserved. No part of this publication may be reproduced, distributed, or transmitted in any form or by any means, including photocopying, recording, or other electronic or mechanical methods, without the prior written permission of the publisher, except in the case of brief quotations embodied in critical reviews and certain other noncommercial uses permitted by copyright law. To obtain permission to excerpt portions of the text, please contact the author at lisareneejones.com. All characters in this book are fiction and figments of the author's imagination.

www.lisareneejones.com

D EAR READERS,

Welcome back to the Damion and Alana story. I know many of you read the fun freebie I did for *Scorned Queen*, but since some of you did not and since it's not available anymore, I've included it as part one in this book. This allows those who have read it to reread or skip to part two which begins at chapter fourteen. It also allows the entire novel to be in one print book—which is available now!

My regular readers know I always like to do a quick recap of the story and how we got to this point, so here we go…

What if you met the love of your life when you were in diapers? Would that make all your dreams come true? When, at only two years old, Alana Blue proclaimed Damion her future husband, she was in love. That love never went away, but young love is delicate and volatile, and Alana somehow had the maturity to see friendship as what mattered. Maybe she was right, maybe she was not, but Damion became her best friend. And despite all the chemistry between them, they stayed just that—friends.

Until the day Damion was to leave for college and decided to kiss her as his goodbye. Only he still had a girlfriend. Alana only kissed him back because she thought they'd broken up. They parted ways as best friends turned enemies, but they were destined to see each other again at Yale.

Somehow though, it was years before they ran into each other, one night at a party. The result was combustible. They ended up in a bedroom, ready to have sex, but then some girl burst into the room looking for Damion, and Alana thought he'd cheated with her on a girlfriend again. Later she'd find out that was not true, but much later.

Flash forward to near graduation time, and Alana is invited to an elite event for the future leaders of New York City. Damion is also invited. She is a mess when she sees him, and when the evening is over, she flees. Damion finds her, and the heat between them is instant. He tells her she was wrong to think he was cheating on the woman who'd shown up when they were at the party. She'd been trying to get with him, and he had eyes for no one but Alana.

Alana goes home with Damion.

In the process, Damion overhears things between Alana and her family via phone calls, and he finds out Alana's father is in gambling debt to the wrong people. The next morning, Damion is gone without saying goodbye, but he's left Alana a note. He's leaving for Europe to run a division of the family business. He's also paid off her father's debt.

Alana then feels like a whore, as if Damion paid for her services. Angry and embarrassed, she rushes to his office and confronts him before he leaves. They part ways on bad terms. Now Damion is gone, and Alana knows it's time to move on with her life, and forget her childhood fantasy of the two of them ending up together.

At this point, Alana has been accepted into Yale and she has her sights on law school. She feels her family needs to diversify their real estate business, and a law degree can help that happen. But then her father slithers his way into more gambling trouble, and she's forced to leave school and help sell the family out of debt. Nothing has gone as she'd planned, not in love nor business.

But then Alana shows a property to a big-time Hollywood person, and suddenly she is being offered her own TV show. This might seem like a dream to many, but she really doesn't want to take it. She isn't a spotlight kind of girl, but her family pressures her to accept the offer. After all, her father is still gambling. Money matters, for all the wrong reasons. Alana caves and takes the offer. Now she's a star, quite literally, as her show is an instant hit.

Then, one night, the studio sends a car for her and a driver transports her to meet a studio head.

Shockingly, it's Damion.

He's the man behind her show.

She's upset but he reminds her she owes him a favor, which only makes her all the angrier, but he's also right. He loaned her family money. He needs a fake fiancée to seal a business deal.

Alana agrees to help Damion, but she still loves him, and it's a struggle to have him touching her and the intimacy between them is as real as it gets. Confessions are made, and she learns he always wanted her, but her friendship rule held him back from pursuing her. He also explains his need to stop his father's brutal business practices and his plan to take over the company.

Alana is all in to help him, even knowing he will break her heart.

There are many revelations that follow, including the way his father is trying to take over her family business because he feels Alana is bad for Damion. He's always been between her and Damion, and it's clear Damion wanted to keep her out of his father's sights, but that just didn't happen. So much so, that it comes to light his father is sleeping with her mother as "payment" for money her father borrowed from Damion's father.

Near the end of the book, Damion gives Alana a ring to make their "fake" engagement look real. This ring is not just any ring, either. It's made of a stone Alana has always loved. Damion confesses that five years ago, he was ready to come back to the States and propose to her. He went so far as to pick out a ring. But he talked himself out of it for a good reason, at least in his mind. He's done things he's not proud of. He's not good for her, and yet he confusingly turns around in the next breath and asks her to move in with him.

Alana's confused and out of sorts, but they head to dinner to meet the CEO this engagement is all about. They are close to sealing a deal with her that helps Damion take over the company when his father shows up, assuring Damion his plan has failed.

And now we begin Scorned Queen…

Part one begins at exactly the next moment after the end of Protégé King.

Lisa

# Part One

# Chapter One

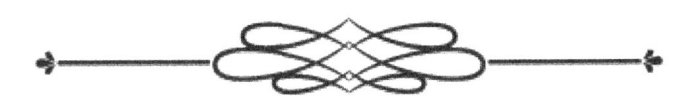

## *Damion*

My father and I stare at each other, and the silent battle we wage on each other is no less fierce than two boxers in the final round of a championship match. Because that's what this is, but the battle is not for a belt, but rather controlling interest of Mary Morrison's company.

My father thinks showing up at the table where Alana and I are wining and dining Mary to win her trust, will destroy my plan to save her company rather than gut it and sell it off, like he would dictate it to the board. It will not. The board is on my side, ready to go from sharks who gut businesses to a company that develops success and takes a piece of the profit for helping it happen in a long-term fashion that ultimately means more profit.

He's a raider, pure and simple, a "man" who makes money by destroying people's dreams and hard work. The worst of it is that I almost let him turn me into his mini me, but no more. I'm not like him. I will not operate on his terms. Never again. "You're not invited, father," I say. "Leave."

"Did you really think members of the board wouldn't tell me you planned to out me?" he asks, all cool and calm, a hint of amusement in his voice. "Did you really think what they said to your face is what they meant? I thought I taught you better."

*The problem for him*, I think, *is they didn't just say it, they signed off on it.* I glance at Mary. "Nothing has changed."

"And yet, it has," she says, shoving her chair back from the table and standing, her long gray hair draping her shoulders. "We're done here." Mary rotates and starts walking.

Alana is already on her feet, tracking Mary with rapid steps, as they both head in the direction of the door. "She can't save Mary for you," my father states, drawing my sharp gaze to his as he adds, "but you can save, Alana."

A chill as icy as an artic breeze slides down my spine at the obvious threat, and I go stiff, doing so because I know things my father has done. Bad things, horrible things, you don't come back from, and he doesn't care.

The fact that my father is sitting here, at this table is meant to panic her and check me. I'm beyond being checked. I'm beyond being caged. Mary is another story. She took his bait, and she ran with it, ready to drown in the muddy waters of his bullshit.

My father thinks he's won, but he hasn't.

Now it's my turn to be amused. I smirk and meet his stare. "Who's going to save you, father?" I ask.

"I thought I already made that clear. The board. You don't own them." He leans in closer. "I do. And you'd be smart not to forget that." He pushes to his feet and walks toward the door.

I don't move. That's what he wants. A reaction.

We both know he's walking toward the door where Alana could end up his target, but despite everything inside me that makes me want to place myself between him and her, it would be a mistake. If I allow him to see her as a delicate creature that I'll protect with a proverbial shield and sword, my father will see blood.

Alana's blood.

And this, right here, this night and the target it's put on Alana's back, is why I stayed away from her, but that ship has sailed. She's mine. And she's strong enough to stand beside me against my father and my enemies. But she needs to believe that herself. That means she needs to know I believe in her.

I force myself to count to twenty and then I flag the waiter and hand him my credit card. I'm cool on the outside, but inside I'm pure fury ready to be unleashed. And if my father steps wrong where Alana is concerned, I'll show him that the cold, ruthless part of me he created isn't dead. It's just waiting on him.

# Chapter Two

## *Alana*

My heart flutters as I race after Mary, desperate to reassure her that Damion is on her side and that he's legitimately eager to aid her quest to save Morrison Enterprises. Adrenaline is not my friend, as my knees wobble a bit, and I worry as much about what is happening between Damion and his father as I do about what's before me with Mary. I don't know what is in the past between them fully, but I remember the way he manipulated and controlled Damion in his youth. I know even if it's been glossed over by Damion, that he became something he isn't proud of, followed in his father's footsteps, and became a version of a man he never wanted to know as himself.

I exit the front door of the restaurant to find Mary standing to my right, her back to me, while she runs fretful fingers through her long, gray hair.

"Mary!" I call out, and rush toward her.

She whirls around, her face etched with shadows, her eyes bloodshot, in a way that tells me the brilliant, tough-as-nails CEO is on the verge of tears. And why wouldn't she be? Damion's father means to rip all her hard work apart and destroy her baby. I've closed the space between us only to have her hold up her hands in a move that reads both protective and defensive. "I have nothing to say to you."

"I swear to you, Damion intends to do right by you. He has the board. This is a manipulation tactic by his father and nothing more. He only wins if we let him win."

"I know Erick, and he's not here to intimidate. He's here to gloat. And the reality here—which I'd like to think you're too naïve to see—is that Damion is his father's son. By luring me into his big plans to save my company, he made me look away. I have no back-up plan."

I reject her point of view as emotional and incorrect. "None of what you just said is true and, on some level, I know you know that. I swear to you—"

"You already said that, Alana. Stop and open your eyes. Damion has a track record of being as cold as his father. Don't marry that man."

"He's not his father," I say without hesitation. "Did he head down that path? Yes. Does he regret it? Yes. I grew up with him. I know him at his core."

"Then why weren't you together until now?"

"Aside from our age?" I ask, but don't wait for an answer. "I forced the friendship thing down Damion's throat. I was so afraid of losing my best friend that I wasn't willing to risk it by dating. He's a good man, and I promise you he's as upset right now as you are. He'll win. His father will not."

"Are you so sure about that?"

At the sound of Damion's father's voice behind me, I go cold, and my eyes meet Mary's, hers filled with warning and a promise: I'm out of my league. He's brutal. I'll get cut and bleed out if I dare stand against him. All of which I reject as surely as I did her assessment of Damion. I don't even think about backing down. "I am," I say, rotating to face him, my chin held high. "And so are you, or you wouldn't be here tonight."

He stuns me then by closing the space between us. We're suddenly toe to toe, his garlic-scented breath fanning my face when he says, "You were always beneath him. That hasn't changed. You were convenient. A fake fiancée to win over the board. They are not impressed any more than I ever was. You're over your head and beneath his stature. Go away, little girl, before you get hurt." With that, he offers me his back and starts walking.

I suck in a breath, and there are pins in my chest, hundreds of pins, pricking my heart, and I am bleeding on the inside in ways only Damion can make me bleed. *Only it's not Damion*, I tell myself. This is his father who hates him, who is trying to hurt him through me, and I cannot let him win.

Mary's hand comes down on my arm and I draw in a calming breath before turning, my eyes meeting hers. "He's not like that man. Do you understand? He is *not like him*."

She studies me with an intense inspection and says softly, "If you still say that after what his father just said to you, I believe you mean those words."

"But you don't believe they're true, do you?"

"Alana."

Damion's voice hums through me, a song in the middle of the scream that is my emotions right now, a salve that soothes the wounds his father has created. I turn to face him, and in an instant, he's in front of me, his hand cupping my face, dark eyes searching my eyes. "What did he say to you?"

I swallow hard. "It doesn't matter. He doesn't matter."

Mary steps into view, beside us both. "He told her she's dirt on your shoe, and you'll never marry her. Do right by us both, Damion, or I swear to you I'll finish this life with you under *my* shoe."

Damion's broad chest rises, stretching the fine silk of his shirt before he replies to what she's said, but he speaks to me instead. "You are everything to me, Alana, even if you don't know it yet, but I swear to you, if it's the last thing I do, you will." And then he ignores the public place and Mary watching, leaning in, his mouth on my mouth, as he kisses me, a deep, seductive slide of his tongue. He tastes like whiskey and forever, but then hasn't he always? At least the forever part?

When his mouth parts mine, I'm breathless, my mind drugged by his kiss, but he's still fully on point, his gaze lifting to Mary's. "I'll do right by you. Because doing right by you is doing right by her."

"I hope you do," she says.

It's right then that her car arrives. She gives me a tiny nod and then walks to the driver's side and climbs inside. A moment later, she is gone, and Damion catches the fingers of one of my hands in his. "Let's go home."

*Home.*

That word choice twists me in knots and pulls tight. He asked me to move in with him, but he also told me the ring on my finger is as fake as his father declared the idea of us marrying. Damion says it's because he's not good enough for me. Then why is he good enough for me to live with?

He tugs me to him, his hand settling low and possessive on my back. "Whatever you're thinking, stop. It's wrong."

I wet my dry lips and nod, but I can't find words.

He kisses my fingers and says, "I'll make you understand."

I nod again, though I don't know what he's referencing.

Make me understand why he can't marry me?

Make me understand why that doesn't matter?

I don't know if either is possible, but not only do I love him, right now, he needs me. And I need him.

# Chapter Three

Damion flags the doorman as he drapes his arm over my shoulders, and pulls me close, his big powerful body warm and strong against mine as we wait for his car. Tonight he's driving a silver Porsche Boxster worth two hundred thousand easily. I can't say the vehicle didn't impress me when he'd unveiled it tonight, because it did, it does, but that level of luxury where Damion is concerned, doesn't surprise me. He's always had money, lots of it, and he's never hesitated to lean into the style and prestige that comes with it. And by his own admission, no matter how vague, he also leaned into the methods his father utilizes to create that wealth. I've heard the stories about his father, the brutal, unethical corporate raider but growing up, he was just Damion's arrogant, grumpy father. I don't like to think about Damion being another version of him, but I do believe him when he says he wants to be a better man. But even with his confession and proclamation, in my mind, it's hard not to think about how I've felt used by Damion at times in our lives, especially after his father came at me like he did.

I've loved him since we were kids, but I've long ago taken off the rose-colored glasses where life, and he, exists.

I've learned that love is a complicated thing. It can both make us whole and shred us, and I fear with Damion, that's the least of my worries. I believe—I *know*—he has the power to carve out my heart and leave me incapable of anything resembling a normal human being. He could easily break me, and I'm not sure I have the same power over him, and that's a problem. A relationship has to be halves, two parts of one whole, and yet equal in who we are and what we are apart and together.

My show might erase my perceived deficiency in career and finances but Damion is why it even materialized. But on the other hand, he gave me an opportunity without guaranteed success. I'm the one who turned it into skyrocketing ratings.

Damion pulls me around in front of him. "I can hear you thinking."

"I'm not surprised. You know me better than anyone on this Earth."

"Then remember the same applies to you with me."

"That's why you picked me for your fake fiancée, right?"

His expression turns stormy. "You know we aren't fake."

"Just the ring?"

"Alana—"

It's right then that the car is pulled up beside us. "We'll talk at your apartment," I say, and someone shoots a photo of me, and I have a piece of paper shoved at me.

"Can I get an autograph, Alana?"

I swallow hard and plant a smile on my lips before greeting the thirty-something woman and scribbling my name on what is actually a napkin, not a piece of paper. A full minute later, I'm warmed by her love of my show, and when she departs, Damion guides me to the car and opens the door. I quickly fold myself into the vehicle, the warm leather enveloping me; much like my love for Damion does every moment I'm with him, but that doesn't make our ride one without turbulence and pain. The truth is, his father's comments were poorly timed, just after the whole ring fiasco. It's real and fake at the same time, which perfectly personifies us.

The entire exchange had cut deep while his father's insults ground in the open wound.

When I would expect the door to shut, Damion kneels beside me, his expression earnest, his eyes troubled as they search my face. There are flutters in my belly with the intensity of his attention. "I'm okay," I whisper as if he's asked a question.

He catches my hand in his and murmurs something I cannot understand, and I'm not sure I'm even meant to understand before he whispers, "Alana," and presses his lips to my knuckles. "I don't believe you, but I'm going to fix it. And us."

And then he's gone, pushing to his feet, and shutting me inside the warm vehicle.

I'm still reeling from whatever that just was, when he climbs inside the driver's side, claiming the captain's seat, so to speak, the earthy scent of him consuming me. They say scent is part of what draws us to another human being. It's a primal thing, beyond our understanding. I can believe that to be true between Damion and me. I'm drawn to him as a man in ways I am not to other men equally good-looking and successful. I have always been drawn to him. I'm not even certain when attraction and friendship became love. Probably very young, and while I didn't understand my feelings back then, I appreciate them more with a little life under my belt. I've learned that a real connection is hard to find.

Damion and I have one.

It's simply failed to lead to a happily ever after between us.

I'm not sure it ever will, and maybe on some deep, instinctual level, I knew it never would, and that's why I insisted so intently on maintaining our friendship. But we've gone beyond that now, and there's no turning back.

# Chapter Four

I BLINK AND WE are on the road, the dark night enveloping us, the passing streetlights flickering through the shadows, tracing the handsome lines of Damion's face. I stare at him, transfixed by his male beauty, and I don't know how one person can cast a spell on another that seems to last an eternity, but isn't that in some ways the definition of happily ever after?

The music permeates my thoughts, an instrumental that needs no words to seduce the listener. "Come Get Her" by Andrew Savoia, has been all over the charts as of late, and I tell myself Damion has done just that. He's come for me. He sought me out. He made my show happen. My finger caresses the engagement ring, and I'm transported back to a day years before.

I'd been seventeen, and obviously Damion not much older, and he'd been forced to attend a wedding at one of his parents' Hampton estates. He'd dreaded the event and begged me to go with him, claiming I'd make it bearable. We'd done that a lot for each other through our teens, always acting as each other's support source.

I shut my eyes and sink deeper into the memory, one not so unlike tonight in many ways.

*Damion and I stand next to an ice sculpture, under some outdoor covering overlooking the ocean, the salty taste in my mouth well doused as I eat icing off his plate. "How do you eat all that sugar?" he asks.*

*"How do you not?" I point my fork at him. "That's the real question."*

*An announcement sounds, and we're all told to claim a seat, for some special dessert. Yes, we had cake before dessert. It's a little weird, but I often don't understand the logic of rich people.*

*Damion grabs both our plates and sets them on a tray before he catches my hand, leading me toward a table. My palm tingles with the connection. Okay, my entire body tingles with the connection. I know he* doesn't think twice about holding my hand—we're best friends—but the girl in me struggles with all the feels it gives me.

Fortunately, the table he's chosen is empty, and we tilt our heads close as I ask, "Who's the bride again?"

"The daughter of one of the board members. She's ten years older than me. I really don't know her."

It's right then that a group of Damion's business club friends sit down, which surprises me because why are they here? Damion reads my mind, leaning in close to whisper, "Alexander's father works with my father. He's dating Christi, the girl with him, and they each brought friends."

I nod, but there's this energy at the table that is electric in all the wrong ways. There are eyes on me and whispers that feel as if they chant my name. Damion exchanges a few words with Alexander, and soon we have some sort of chocolate bonbons on a plate placed in front of us. Damion eyes me. "I know you love this."

I grin. "What makes you think that?"

"Which one first?"

It's a game we play, tasting new things at the same time. "The round one." We reach for them together and take a bite. Damion immediately makes a face.

"That is not good," he says.

I laugh and finish the entire thing. "I disagree." But even as I do, there's this weird tingling sensation on my nape that has me glancing up to find Alexander staring at me.

I swallow hard, with the intensity of his attention.

"You're that real estate agent family, right?"

I fight the urge to pop back and remind him one person is not a family, but I never get the chance. His head snaps to Damion and he says, "Man, what is she doing here?"

My cheeks heat, and I feel as if quicksand is all around me, and my chair might as well be sinking into the deep, dark, muddy water. Damion's fingers curl in his palms a moment, and I can almost feel him battling his anger, which is only going to make this worse. I grab his leg and squeeze, whispering, "Please don't."

But there is no "don't" to be had. Damion scoots his plate aside and says, "Leave my table, Alexander, and do not even think about sitting with me again.

Alexander pales. "What?"

"You heard me," Damion bites out. "Leave now."

"I meant no harm, Damion."

"And yet, you caused it," he says.

The two of them stare at each other for several beats and then to my utter shock, Alexander motions to his girlfriend and the lot of them stand and leave. It's then that I realize how much power Damion possesses. I mean I knew, I did, but I've never seen it on display, not like this. I'm mortified at what has just happened, and I try to stand up.

Damion catches my hand, and when my eyes meet his, the punch between us is created by years of friendship, and something more, something that is as confusing as it is painful. "I need to go to the bathroom."

"Don't go."

"I just—" I swallow, "I need a minute."

He fills his lungs with a heavy breath, his broad, perfect chest expanding beneath his crisp, white shirt. I'm wearing a pink dress he'd called sweet. He's in a suit I'd called brutal. Somehow, that now fits but is also unfair. He's just protecting me, I know he is. I know that's his intent.

"Damion," I whisper, a plea for him to release me.

A heavy breath lifts his chest, and he runs the fingers of his free hand through his thick, dark hair before he releases me. I'm cold in an instant, which only sends me rushing toward the house all the faster. There are bathrooms there, and while they are probably for the elites, not people like me, I pray for a moment of privacy. I tilt my chin low, and hurry though what must be a crowd of three hundred. Once I'm inside the house, which is a monstrous white mansion that would fit five of my houses, I hurry up the stairs to an area where a map indicated a powder room.

Thankfully, at the top of the landing the door is open, and I step inside.

"Alana!"

At the sound of Damion's voice, I step back into the hallway.

"Don't do this," he says, joining me, all but touching me again. "Don't hide away and act as if you don't belong. You'll get into an ivy league school because of your brains. He'll get in because of his parents' money. That makes you better than him."

"I don't want to be better than him, Damion," I proclaim. "I just want to be the best me, and to not be looked down on. And I know you were trying to protect me, but I'm embarrassed about all of it. I don't want to be here like this."

"Like what?"

"Like decoration."

"It's not like that," he says tightly, but we both know it is, proven by the way his hand drags through his hair once again before both his hands land on his waist. "Fuck this party. Let's go down to the beach and pick *up those seashells you love."* He motions to the bathroom. *"Go pee. You always have to pee. Then we're getting out of here."*

I blink back to the present, streetlights, flickering past my window. *And we had*, I think. We'd gotten out of there. We'd gone to the beach and laughed over bon bons and two desserts, and the world had been right again. But deep down, we'd both known we were from two different worlds, and one day our roads would lead us two different directions. Maybe that's why we never kissed until the day he left for college. It was easier to say goodbye that way.

I glance over at him, his strong profile in the thick darkness of the vehicle as he navigates toward his apartment. He wants me to move in with him, but how do I do that when there is still a divide? He'll live with me but not marry me. It reads like me getting hurt again. And I'm just not sure I'm built sturdy enough to do that again, not with Damion.

# Chapter Five

I BLINK AGAIN AND we are already pulling up to Damion's apartment. *Our apartment,* if Damion has his way. But is his way my way? Not the way things are now. Not yet. I'm confused by what is happening between us. And I'm afraid of losing me in this process of finding out, and me having a solid handle on my own identity and goals has always been what saved me from brutal heartache where Damion's concerned. Not that my identity has become what I'd strived for it to be, but I'm pretty darn grateful for where I've landed. I've come to a point where I'm not giving Damion the credit for my show as I was when I first found out he'd opened that door for me. I mean, in business, connections matter. I learned that way back in college when I was already mixing and mingling with the rich and famous, as they judged me worthy or not worthy of a future proverbial crown. Damion opened the door for me, yes, but I've done the camera work. I've made the show mine and I'm proud of what I've created. I've also held my family together most of my adult life. That took sacrifice and courage.

I glance over at Damion to find him staring at me. "What are you thinking?" he asks.

His eyes are filled with concern, and my heart squeezes at the uncertainty I read in him. I am probably, almost definitely the only person on this Earth he allows himself to be vulnerable with, because uncertainty is vulnerability, or so they taught me at Yale. And so his father taught him his entire life. But the issue here isn't how easy it is for him to be vulnerable with me.

It's how that becomes uncertainty.

And he *is* uncertain about me. That's why the ring isn't real, and he wants me to move in with him, not marry him. Maybe on some level he really does know our two worlds were never meant to be one. And yet, somehow, they have never been more interlinked and far apart than they are right this minute.

Damion will never intentionally hurt me. He just can't help himself.

The door opens beside me, and when I would escape and avoid his question I'm not quite ready to answer, Damion catches my arm and pulls me around to him. His fingers press against my arm, and even through my jacket, the heat of his touch sizzles up my arm and across my chest. "What are you thinking?" he presses.

I'm drowning in the intensity of his dark eyes, swimming in a pool of lust and love that will soon be the end of me. I feel it in every part of me, but I also feel him. I feel him in every possible way, inside and out. "That you're going to shred my heart before this is over, and I'm still going upstairs with you."

"I would never—"

"And yet, you always do."

"Alana," he breathes out, his voice as rough as sandpaper and yet it's still silk on my nerve endings. Everything about him is sandpaper and silk. I believe that's part of what makes him so ridiculously dangerous.

"Take me upstairs," I whisper.

A tormented look flashes in his eyes. "This conversation isn't over."

I nod because agreement is the only way he'll release me, of this I'm certain. He studies me another beat, seeming to weigh my headspace, surely not about to pass his inspection. And yet, almost accepting of this fact, he reluctantly releases me. We both know we won't talk when we get upstairs. We'll fuck like rabbits and fall asleep. And that's probably for the best. Morning light always brings clarity an emotional night does not. I think we can both use a good dose of sex and morning light clarity.

# Chapter Six

I EXIT THE CAR, and I swear Damion is there before it's physically possible, an impatience in the way he palms a large bill to the bellman. I might not have been sleeping with Damion for a very long time, but I know him like I know my own smell. He needs an outlet. He needs to be inside me. And after what his father said to me, as far as I'm concerned, that's such a better way to cope with this night, than conversation.

I don't want to think about what transpired with his father. I sure as heck don't want to talk about it. I just want to get lost in Damion, and some part of me is aware I won't have him for long. A big part of me believes I won't and believes he feels the same of me. How can he not? Can *we* not? We're always two steps from losing each other, but we have always found our way back together.

But then we'd never crossed that line and slept together, either.

Damion catches me to him, his arm sliding around my lower back, palm settling on my opposite hip, his hard, warm, big body aligned to mine. There's an intimacy to the way he holds me; sensual, possessive. I've never known him to be someone who is about public displays of affection, but tonight he kissed me in front of Mary, and now he's all but telling the entire building we're about to have sex. And me—little, always conservative me—doesn't even care. I'm drugged by his touch, my mind muddled up by the awareness working its way through every part of my body.

We approach the building, and the sliding doors open, allowing us to enter. I'm immediately aware of a thirty-something man in a suit with a buzz cut and a hard-set jaw standing near the desk. His entire presence screams ex-military-turned-security, which means he watches everyone and sees everything and I'm instantly wondering what he must think of us. Wondering what he must think of *me*. It's not something I wonder for long as Damion halts us in front of him, and the surprise I feel at this move is echoed in this stranger's eyes.

My cheeks heat and I am instantly self-conscious as he motions between me and the stranger. "Noah, meet Alana. Alana, Noah."

Noah's attention lands on me, the surprise in his eyes deepening, as both of us are clearly wondering what the heck is happening right now.

"Welcome, Alana," Noah greets and there is a flicker in his eyes of something I cannot name but I wish I could, because I feel like he's more in the know right now than I am.

"Thank you," I say uneasily.

"Noah's the head of security for the building," Damion explains and then addresses Noah directly, "Alana is moving in with me and she's become quite the star. She has a TV show and—"

I blanch at this announcement Damion and I have not yet confirmed, then blanch again as Noah says, "I'm aware. My sister is unemployed and watches it all the damn time."

I'm taken aback by Noah's admission, aware now that look in his eyes was about my show, not me moving in with Damion, and his reference to his sister in the mix manages to drag a laugh out of me. "I take it you don't like my show?"

"I'd like your show a whole lot more if she were employed and out of my house."

I laugh again, finding him remarkably likable considering the hardness he oozes. "I understand. We'll be in reruns soon. Maybe that will help."

"She'll just watch the Hallmark Channel," he mutters and then adds, "but welcome to the building, Alana. It's not your fault my sister is lazy." He eyes Damion and then me. "It's nice to see him settling down."

This remark flutters about in my belly like butterflies, and then nose dives into anger at the pure manipulation of the moment. "I've known him a very long time."

His brow lifts. "Really? And I've never seen you before, why?"

I twist out of Damion's grip and point a finger at him that is an accusation in all kinds of ways even if my tone is not. "I think he struggled with the idea that I'd seen him in diapers," I say, because giving Damion a hard time is something I've practiced most of my life.

Damion laughs now. "As I have you, Alana."

I'm not happy with him right now, but it's impossible not to feel the connection between us and the heat of his body without a bit of an internal sigh. "We're going to call it a night, Noah," Damion says, capturing my hand with his and then tugging me closer, his arm sliding back around me, even as he adds, "If you need me, you know how to reach me."

"Indeed," Noah agrees and gives me a nod. "Goodnight and nice to meet you, Alana."

"Nice to meet you, Noah."

Damion rotates us away from Noah and toward the elevator, and that's when my anger really begins to truly ignite. In an effort to calm myself and remain logical, I mentally replay what just happened. My conclusion is that while I want this man to want me, and yes, *I want* him, everything about what just happened speaks of the layers of complication between us.

We halt at the elevator, and I can feel my body vibrating with my hyped-up emotions. Damion punches the button, and the doors open instantly. I twist out of his arms and step into the car, and I hate the way his touch has left me smoldering in the aftermath. I just want him to touch me again, but isn't that the problem? He has seduced me far too easily all my life.

I can feel him at my back, his energy, his body heat, and my mind is already muddled with his nearness. I rotate to face him, trying to regain my control, of which, I have little with Damion. He punches the key to his floor, and it *is his* floor, not mine, contrary, of course, to what he just told Noah. I haven't made the decision to move in with him and he doesn't get to make it for me. The doors shut and now Damion and I are facing each other, the energy between us cracking and snapping.

"Why are you over there?" he demands, and proceeds to move my direction.

I hold up a hand, then a finger. "Wait. I'm pissed at you, and we both know there are cameras in these elevators. I don't want either of us to be fodder for the press."

His chin lowers, eyes burning into mine. "Alana," he says softly.

"Don't say my name like you're scolding me, Damion. I'm not your employee. Or maybe I am." I lift my hand with the ring.

"Employee," he repeats, his tone sharp with anger. "Are you fucking kidding me?"

"That's what I want to say to you right now, but since this video could be played on TMZ, minus volume, and our body language analyzed, I'm not."

"You think they can't read us right now? Come over here and make nice for the camera."

"I'll stand next to you but do not touch me or I will not be responsible for my actions."

His lips hint at amusement, I dare him to make more obvious, but he gives me a nod. We move at the same time, stepping close and rotating to face the front of the elevator. I wait for him to touch me, to push me, like he did with Noah, and if he does, if he disrespects my wishes, it will be the end of this night. But he doesn't. Really, he doesn't get the chance. The doors open almost instantly, and I step into the hallway, pausing to wait on him.

He joins, six foot two inches of sexy, arrogant man, and for a moment we just stand there and stare at each other, a push and pull between us that is blazing physical attraction pumped up by a punch of white lightning anger. He draws in a breath, and motions with his head toward his apartment. I give a barely-there nod and in unison, we walk toward his door, the air charged around us. There's an explosion coming of epic proportions, and the only chance I have of winning this battle is by keeping my clothes on. Because if we end up naked, he is absolutely on top.

And we both know it.

# Chapter Seven

Damion unlocks his door but doesn't open it, and before I know his intention, he pulls me in front of him, forcing me to catch my weight on my hands, and the door. I'm officially caged between it and the man who'd I'd call my biggest temptation, and at present, the source of my ire. Not exactly the way to maintain my control, especially when his powerful thighs and hips frame my backside, one of his palms pressed to my waist, the other over my head, on the wooden surface.

"I'm crazy about you," he murmurs, his lips near my ear, his breath tantalizingly warm, lips brushing my neck.

My knees are weak, and my body is one big nerve ending that is alive and charged.

"You treated me like an employee," I hiss.

He turns me to face him, his eyes glistening with his own anger now. "I treated you like the woman I want in my life."

My lashes lower and my lips tremble, and I fight all the things I want to say to him, that only make me look as foolish as I have often felt with Damion. But I can't hold it all back…I just can't. When I look at him again, I say, "For how long this time?"

"There's never been a time in my life that I didn't want you with me."

"And yet, there's been so much of it you made sure we spent apart."

"It's not like that, Alana." He caresses hair from my face. "You—"

Voices sound behind us and he curses, his arm wrapping my waist to steady me before he opens the door. "Let's go inside," he says softly, and I don't fight him. I twist around and away from him, away from the intimacy of his touch that makes me as wet as it does dumb.

By the time I've rotated to face him, he's shut the door and he's standing closer than I'd like, a predatory gleam in his eyes. "Alana—"

"What was that down there?" I demand, my finger pointing at the ground.

"I was removing any thought you had that I didn't really want you to move in with me."

"I didn't have that thought," I say, when I want to confront him about the way he plays with my emotions. Giving me the ring and telling me it was bought for me, but that he'd changed his mind about coming home to get me. Now it's mine, but it means nothing. It's a callous thing to do for personal gain. It's almost cruel. But if I say that, I seem like a pathetic girl in love with the rich boy next door who is still too good for her. "This wasn't about me thinking you didn't want me, Damion. That—what you did—was manipulation, which feels a whole lot like a family trait."

He draws in another heavy breath and for several seconds he just stands there before he huffs out that air and scrubs his hand through the thick strands of his dark hair. It's an act of frustration, something he rarely shows, at least not with others, but he can't hold back with me and I'm not sure what that says about us. All I know is that I feel like nothing more than the sum of an acting gig as his fake fiancée.

His cellphone rings and he says, "I need a drink."

He ignores the call and walks toward the bar. I hug myself, a sharp stab of guilt in my belly. I shouldn't have said that to him. "Damion," I say, taking a step toward him.

He holds up a hand without ever even looking at me. "Not now, Alana."

My chin dips to my chest with the rejection I deserve. I'm hurt and I lashed out and I've seen how that works for my parents. It destroys relationships. And Damion and I aren't kids anymore who can scream at each other one minute and just go play outside the next. Life is far more complicated as adults. *We're* far more complicated.

I walk toward the floor-to-ceiling window again, bringing in the glint and glitter of the stars and city light blurred by a heavy cloud cover. A storm is coming, and it's not just the weather. It's me and Damion. It's him and his father. It's me and my family.

I'm just wildly confused about what is happening between me and Damion, while he appears wildly uncertain. I stare down at the gorgeous ring he gave me. We'd been right here in this spot, and I squeeze my eyes shut, replaying the memory, trying to find the truth of me and him, in the memory...

*He reaches in his pocket and produces a velvet box, and before I can react, he says, "You can't be a fiancée without a ring."*

*There's a pinch of disappointment in my chest. This is not real. Of course, it's not real.* "Okay," I murmur.

He opens the lid and a stunning, heart-shaped diamond glistens and glows inside. My gaze jerks to Damion. "I used to love hearts as a kid." I laugh but it sounds choked, even to my ears. "It's kind of appropriate but it seems extravagant for a fake fiancée, Damion."

"Because it wasn't meant for a fake fiancée, Alana. Five years ago, I got drunk and decided I could come back and get you. I chose the hearts because you always had them everywhere. You even drew them on me at one point."

I can barely breathe. I can barely speak. "I—I don't understand. We hadn't talked and—"

He catches my chin and leans in and kisses me, his lips lingering against mine for long moments even after the kiss ends. "This is me telling you, Alana, I meant what I said earlier. I might not have said it until tonight, but you have always been it for me. Always."

My heart swells, and I feel what I can almost call a sense of completion. Like he is a part of me I was missing, and now he's here but I'm afraid to believe it's true. I don't really even understand what this is or why he's saying it. I can feel more coming, and I find myself holding my breath, not sure what to expect.

"But you also need to know that the morning after I bought this ring, Alana, I came to my senses. I knew I was not good for you. I know it now, too, but when you're standing in front of me, I can't seem to give a damn. I am not good for you. You need to remember that. And if I get drunk and propose again, be smart and say no." He cups my face. "And stop being stubborn and move in with me."

My heart is happy and my brain a bit drunk on this conversation. "Why does it always feel as if you are standing in front of me but out of reach?"

"Because I'm always trying to protect you from me."

"Alana."

My eyes open to find Damion standing in front of me offering me a glass of whiskey. "I thought we could both use the strong stuff."

It's insane the way my heart leaps with his nearness, the way butterflies dance in my belly when I've known him my entire life. I accept the glass, the brush of our fingers jolting me, and I think I see the same reaction in his eyes. Or maybe, I just want to see the same in his eyes. I down the amber liquid, choking with the bite of the liquor. It's warm in my belly and my apology is fast on my tongue. "I'm sorry. I should have never said that to you."

He tips his own drink back, emptying the contents of the glass before he sets it on the wide steel ledge separating the window. He takes mine and does the same. The buzz in my head is officially here and I laugh without humor. "That was not a good idea. I'm already feeling whatever it was I just drank. Damion, I—"

He catches me to him, and the feel of him next to me is everything. His touch warms me all over. His smell permeates my senses and stirs emotions and wild flutters in my belly. He maneuvers me backward and leans me against the steel beam that flows from floor to ceiling, one hand warm on my hip, the other on the beam above my head, torment in the depth of his stare.

"I did what I did because I felt the push between us. I knew you were going to say yes, and I want you to say yes."

"Then talk to me," I say. "Don't—"

He catches my hand with the ring and holds it between us. "I know this is about this ring. Isn't it?"

I blanch with the directness of his words, a deer in headlights. What do I even say to him right now? I don't know what to say. You hurt me. You won't marry me. Why would anyone want a man to marry them if they didn't want to marry them? I don't. Not even Damion. Especially not Damion.

So I'm back to what I always do with him—living in the moment and with the heat of the booze and the heat of his body burning through me, it's not a hard thing to do. Exactly why I say, "Can you just kiss me already?"

# Chapter Eight

"Alana," he murmurs softly, and my name on his lips is more dangerous than whiskey to my good sense. I'm drunk on his very existence.

"Damion," I whisper in reply, and while my name on his lips had been all about heat and fire, his name on mine is every question I have but don't dare speak.

As if he reads that in me, his hand closes around the ring and my hand. "This isn't nothing."

"It's fake," I reply, when in my mind I've told myself to just let it go, but apparently, I just don't have that in me.

"It's not fake. God, woman. I bought it *for you*."

*Only to basically tell me it was a stupid mistake*, I think, but this isn't a conversation I want to have right now. My emotional bandwidth has expired times a thousand. I try to push around him. He cages my legs with his powerful thighs. "Alana." This time my name is stubborn plea. He's not ready to drop this, and I am.

"Let me go."

"I did that several times now," he replies "It never works out for me."

"I don't even know what that means."

"Letting you get away was a mistake I won't make again."

The words are sweet, like sugar and happiness, but they don't compute with everything else he's said and done. "You confuse me."

"Says the woman who told me we could only be friends when we both wanted more."

"Okay," I admit. "That's fair, but we were kids. We're *not kids anymore*."

"We're not just friends either." He releases my hand and grips my waist, and I swear his hand on my body is already burning through my brain cells. His forehead presses to mine, and he murmurs, "I did things, Alana." His voice radiates with a mix of guilt and torment. And while no, this is not the first time he's said something like this to me, there's a gut-wrenching quality to his confession that tears down the wall the whole ring thing has slammed between us.

My hand presses to his cheek, and I meet his stare, my hope that he sees the truth in my eyes. "Whatever you did, it's in the past. I don't care."

"I do," he insists. "I care. I don't want you to know *those* things, and my worst fear is that I might not be able to hide them from you."

"I don't need you to hide anything from me, Damion. That feeling—like you need to do that—it's not us. That's not who I want to believe we are together. And that's not how we make this work."

"It might be the *only* way we make this work."

"You want to live with someone you have to keep secrets from? Really? That's your idea of happy? The person you live your life with should be able to deal with the good, the bad, and the ugly. It's not like my family doesn't have its ugly."

"It's not the same, Alana."

"It's the same to me."

"No." His expression tightens. "It wouldn't be if you knew the details, which you will not."

"That doesn't work for me, Damion."

"Try harder to make it work," he demands.

Anger churns in my belly and I try once again to escape his embrace. I barely move. He's too big and too strong for me to push myself out of this confrontation.

"I thought I could protect you by staying away, but that didn't work," he confesses. "My father still has his claws in your family. I need you close, but I don't know how close I dare."

"Living with you is pretty close."

"Probably too close, but I *need* to be able to protect you."

That's twice he's made that statement and this time, I bristle and press my hand to his chest. "Is that what this is? A way to protect me?"

He covers my hand with his. "*You know better*. Do you really think I'd give you that ring and tell you the story behind it if I didn't want to marry you, Alana? If I didn't want to see the look in your eyes when I told you what I'd wanted then, and what I have always wanted with you."

"And what did you see, Damion? What do you see now?"

"A woman who doesn't believe I'll be here tomorrow."

"Will you?"

"I need to know nothing can blow back on you."

My gut twists in painful knots. "That's not the answer I want, and most importantly, it's not the answer I need to be able to say yes to living with you. It sounds like an excuse."

"It's not a damn excuse. I'm standing here, right here, right now, telling you it's bigger than that, Alana. It's *so damn much more.*"

In that moment, it's easier for me to believe he's afraid of what I might learn than afraid of a real future with me. Maybe because it's true. Maybe because it's what I want to believe. "The part where I'm not the little girl next door anymore just doesn't seem to compute with you and maybe it never will."

"No," he says, "you're not the little girl next door. You're the woman I want in my bed every day when I wake up."

He shrugs out of his jacket, and everything inside me screams, "Yes, please, let's stop talking. Let's get naked." My sex clenches, and there is this need inside me for this man that has existed for what feels like my entire life. It's pure craving, and that craving doesn't care about heartache, rings, business agreements, or even living arrangements.

I reach for his silver tie and tug it free, the silk pooling on the ground as surely as I'm melting in my own high heels.

His hands settle possessively on my hips, scorching me right through the thin black silk of my blouse. There's possessiveness in the way he holds me, the air charges around us, and my knees tremble with the intensity of what I share with this man. "God, woman," he murmurs. "What do you do to me and how do you do it over and over and *over* again? *Tell me.*" But he doesn't give me the chance to argue the reality, which is much different than his version of who does what.

In my world, it's him who messes with my head and emotions.

Him who always leaves.

Or maybe it's not like that at all.

I don't know if I'm objective right now.

He shifts our lower bodies, melding us intimately close, hips to hips, and I am breathless with the press of his thick erection against my belly. My teeth worry my bottom lip. What am I doing with Damion again? Why am I offering my heart up for destruction again? "I should run away," I whisper.

"Yes," he says. "You should. But don't." He catches the hem of the black silk and his warm fingers press to the delicate skin beneath it.

He's all man now, confident and sure of what he wants, a man who gets what he wants, and I've always admired those traits in him. In contrast, I've always known what I wanted, but nothing I swore I'd make happened, happened. I'm not an attorney. I'm not his wife. Not that you make marriage happen, but then I never thought that's how it would go. I just thought we'd end up together, like that's what the universe had in store for us.

Damion leans in closer and presses his cheek to my cheek, his lips to my ear. "Stop thinking whatever you're thinking." He eases back, his dark eyes meeting mine. "We've been through hell, but we found our way back to each other."

His fingers caress a path over my skin until he's pulling my blouse over my head and tossing it aside, his gaze raking over my nearly naked breasts. "Have I told you how many times I've fantasized about you, Alana?" he murmurs, his finger teasing my nipple where it puckers beneath the barely-there lace.

A heavy breath trembles from my lips with the clench of my sex. I'm struggling to remember why this is a bad idea, why *we* are a bad idea, and already Damion is unhooking my bra, dragging it away. "Did you fantasize about me, too, Alana?"

His fingers tease my nipples and my throat is almost too dry for words—almost—and yet somehow, I manage the truth. "I was too busy hating you to dream about you."

His palms are back on my waist. "Liar. You don't hate me."

"It was easier than loving you, Damion. It hurt less."

Seconds tick by as he weighs my words, and I can see his own hatred in his eyes. Hatred for my words, hatred for the truth in them, hatred of himself and this moment of truth. Then suddenly, he turns me to face the pillar, forcing me to catch my weight on the steel, and for reasons I can't explain, I feel as cold as its surface, only my cold is inside, where it's lived a very long time.

He unzips my skirt and drags it down my hips and gives my backside a smack. I yelp, and my heart is racing when he turns me back around, and now I'm in nothing but thigh highs, heels, and panties with Damion's hand on the steel bar above my head.

"I deserve your hate," he says. "I earned it. But that seems like a really good reason for me to give you about a dozen orgasms and you to let me do it."

# Chapter Nine

Let him give me a dozen orgasms.

The deliciousness of his exaggerated concept, and even more so the act of making it so, might not solve anything, but I don't care. We're here, right here, right now, and the miles that still remain between us can't divide us, at least not while we're focused on pleasure and orgasms. I don't want to think about secrets and class wars, and where we fit together or don't fit at all, based on those things. There's enough whiskey in me to be all about momentary gratification, no matter the fleeting bliss it might create.

"You've always been good at talking big," I murmur, aware of the challenge in those words. "You owe me a dozen orgasms, and I'll allow you one week to deliver."

He leans in close, his lips just above mine, his breath oh, so perfectly warm against my skin. "How about one a day, and you agree to stay one year—three hundred and sixty-five days—and then I'll talk you into staying another." His lips brush mine, and I feel the connection in every part of me.

"You get a weekend and a dozen orgasms," I counter. "If you can't keep that promise, why would I stay a year?"

His lips curve with a low chuckle and he says, "All right. I'll start with a weekend."

"Is this where you finally shut up and kiss me?" I challenge.

"Yes, baby," he murmurs, "this is definitely when I shut up and kiss you." And even before he makes good on that promise, I'm reveling in the endearment. *Baby.* It's nothing really, I know, spoken by many a man, in many a casual situation, but somehow it manages to shut out our childhood and take us to a place where we are man and woman with needs and wants that include each other.

I've barely materialized that thought when his tongue finds mine, licking deliciously into my mouth, and every part of me responds, every part of me tingles. The kiss is the same bittersweet perfection that personifies Damion in every possible way. Just as he desires to lock me down, be it for one weekend, one week, or one year. There is never forever with Damion. The idea has me leaning into the freedom that represents. We aren't forever, but we are right now. That's where my head has to stay with Damion. I know this. I've always known this.

My fingers dive into the thick, dark strands of his hair, and when his mouth parts mine, his teeth scrape my lips. "I'm going to lick every part of you before this night is over."

"Promises, promises," I murmur. "So much talk." But even as I say the words, there's a shift in the air between us from playful to serious.

He leans in and kisses my neck, and I swear his lips are velvet that travel to my shoulder, and it's only now that I am suddenly aware of the fact that I'm naked and he is not. He says I know him, and I do. I know exactly why he wanted it this way. It's all about his control, of which he feels he has none right now, because I won't just say yes to a weekend, a week, a year, that might not be another year. But I don't care if he has control of my body. I have control of my mind, and my heart has to take a backseat in decision making.

Damion's phone rings again and with a grimace, he snatches it from his pocket, the caller ID in view, *King Asshole*, it reads. He declines the call, and I catch his hand. "Do you need—"

He leans in and kisses me until my toes curl before he declares, "You. I need *you*, Alana, and if you want to talk about hate, I hate how much you don't know that." He pulls up his music app and pushes play. He set his cell on the steel railing next to me, and music fills the room, an easy invitation to block out the rest of the world.

Damion curls me into him, his hands caressing up and down my back, and it's hard not to feel tiny and vulnerable folded against him, but somehow this arouses me. He's always been that dominant male persona that I liked a bit too much, and I'm not sure what that says about me. His hands press to my breasts, his mouth to my mouth, and then he's lifting me and leaning me against that steel beam all over again.

He kisses me and then lowers his head, his mouth suckling my nipple, and the room fades but the song does not. It's "Astronaut in an Ocean" by Masked Wolf, and the words have me trying to escape the whirlwind of emotion they stir in me, digging my fingers in his hair and willing his mouth to mine. Instead, he palms my breasts, and the words haunt me.

*When these people talk too much, put that shit in slow motion, yeah. I feel like an astronaut in the ocean.*

I've always felt like an astronaut in an ocean when I'm inside Damion's world, out of place and yet where I belong when it's just me and him. But it isn't just me and him. There are so many other people involved. Finally, his mouth is on mine, and he tastes like whiskey, power, and torment, as if he's certain he'll lose me, and I'm not sure what to do with that information nor does he give me time to go that deep.

He cups my face and says, "You're thinking too damn much. Obviously, I'm not doing my job."

"Am I a job now?"

"Don't turn that around on me. It's every man's job to take care of his woman, and you are my woman, Alana."

I could tell him I'm not his woman, but the words don't come to me. He eases me down his body, and my feet touch the ground, and we just stare at each other. "No objection to being called my woman?"

"It crossed my mind, but it would be a lie for me to deny the truth. And I'm pretty sure I was just preaching about honesty, even if we didn't use that word. I've been your woman for the entirety of my adult life."

His eyes burn like blue fire before he kisses the hell out of me and then scoops me up and starts walking.

# Chapter Ten

Damion's bed is every bit what you'd expect a king's bed to be, larger than life, with towering posts I don't remember really giving thought to until tonight. Because tonight, as he sets me on my feet, he leans me against that thick wooden surface and says, "This is where you belong." One of his hands is on my hip, a possessive burn to that touch, while the other is on the wood above my head. "That ring—"

Everything in my head screams in rejection of what he might say next. I've officially turned this night into me playing the role of the desperate girl who wants to marry the guy who doesn't want to get married. It's embarrassing and not who I want to be. "No," I say, my hand pressing to his chest, the act pausing his words, and I can feel his heart thundering beneath my palm. "Don't talk about the ring." I pull it from my hand and press it into his. "Now, can we just forget the ring and fuck already?"

His spine stiffens, and he stands ramrod still. He is stone, unmoving, his expression impenetrable, a tic in his jaw, and yet the sexual tension between us still crackles like electricity. Seconds pass, and the silence mixed with my boldness becomes my enemy, and just when I'm about to act or say something, anything, he catches my hand and slides the ring back into place.

And when his eyes meet mine, he says, "We can fuck all night long as long as this ring is on your finger."

There's no time for me to react or even assess what I feel right now. His hand slides under my hair, his palm to my neck, pulling my naked body flush to his. "You really have no idea how much I want you, or how much I have always wanted you, do you?" It's a question filled with torment and self-hate, that I don't quite understand. His mouth closes over on mine, his tongue stroking into my mouth, wicked and full of demand, the whiskey and power I'd tasted minutes before has transformed to torment, hunger, and need mixed with a possessiveness that says he believes he's about to lose me. The truth is I'm his to lose.

I'm not really sure what that means for him or me, but my arms fold around him, and I offer myself to him, a shelter in the wildness of a storm I believe has raged in him far longer than I ever imagined. And right now, he needs someplace to put it all. He needs me. And I need him. But there must be something he tastes on my lips, in my reaction, in the way I'm responding to him, that undoes him, because he tears his mouth from mine.

He presses me against the bedpost again, a mix of dark passion and shadows in the depth of his eyes that I can only call haunting, but he says nothing. I say nothing. But then the time for words has long passed, and the burn of possession and the need for control radiates from him. The charge between us is a live wire, and when his gaze rakes over my naked breasts, my nipples pucker and my sex clenches. I ache to feel him press inside me, to fill me, and yet still he just stares at me, one second more. I reach for his shirt. He catches my wrist, his grip snug but not painful.

"One day you'll run away just like you said you should in the living room."

He's afraid, I realize now. Afraid for me to see the truth of who he is, and that's almost impossible for me to wrap my head around. This is me he fears, not some stranger, but I say the words I know he needs to hear, "What if I don't? And will you ever know, if you keep pushing me away?"

"You think you can handle it."

"I know I can."

His eyes narrow, darken to almost black, and then he presses my hands to the post behind me and says, "Let's see what you can really handle. Show me you trust me. Do what I say and nothing else."

We're back to his need for power, and my need to give it to him, which I'll analyze in the morning. "Okay then," I say.

He steps back from me, no longer touching me, the very act of him standing there, fully dressed, and me here naked, hugging a pole, and not him, as submissive and arousing as anything I've ever known.

My chin lifts. "Now what?" I whisper.

"Keep your hands right there. Understand?"

I wet my parched lips and nod, warm all over, my nipples rock-hard pebbles. "Yes," I whisper.

"Good," he replies, and I am rewarded for my compliance as he reaches for the buttons on his shirt. Finally, he will be naked with me, and true to that expectation and hope, a moment later his shirt is open enough that he's tugging it over his head. He tosses it aside, the flex of muscle and man a delicious answer to my compliance. But just when I hope and hunger for him to fully undress, he closes the space between us.

Instinct has me reaching for him, and he catches my hands and presses them back against the bedpost. "I told you, baby, *don't move.*"

Somehow there is a contrast of tenderness and command in his voice that is as arousing and confusing as everything else about Damion. "Or else what?" I ask, daring a bold question that pulls us deeper in this power play.

His hands settle on my waist, fire against my skin, and he leans in close, his warm breath a fan on my neck as he says, "I'll be forced to punish you."

For some odd reason, my belly trembles with this promise, and it's all I can do not to touch him. I don't know this part of Damion, but I'm not afraid as I suspect he thinks I will be. I'm not even a little afraid. "How?" I ask instead.

I can feel him smile against my skin a moment before he eases back and says, "I'll spank you, Alana. And I'll enjoy it, as will you. So feel free to break the rule. Move your hands. Give me a reason to turn you over my lap."

# Chapter Eleven

The little girl in me that grew up next door to Damion wants to laugh at his promise to turn me over his lap, but he's not laughing at all, and I have no idea why I'm suddenly ten times hotter than I was moments before. I've never done such a thing in my life. Never had a man touch me as he suggests he will or talk to me in such a way. I feel young and naïve and really quite vanilla when we are nearly the same age. But then, I remind myself that I was never really all in with anyone in my life, *but Damion*.

Either way, I don't know what I feel right now, or what his intent is behind such an erotic statement, but it doesn't feel as simple as it seems.

"Have you ever been spanked, Alana?" he asks, and it's a question meant to push me, maybe scare me away even, if he were honest. In one breath, he says he wants me to stay. In another, he pushes me away, but I think of the torment I've tasted in his kiss and seen in his eyes, and I know he really wants me to stay.

But he needs to know I can see him for who he is, be it the boy next door, or the future king of Wall Street, and everything in between. This is all about his "you can't handle it" declaration.

"You'd be my first," I confess. "First kiss, first spanking. It fits, right?" My chin lifts in defiance. "But you'll have to make me move my hands to make that happen."

Satisfaction lights his dark eyes and he answers me not with words but with actions, his hand closing around the silk between my legs as he tears it from my body. I yelp with the shock of the action, and it's almost enough for me to move my hands, his intent I'm sure, but I do not. His fingers press between my legs, stroking the wet heat of my sex, his lips curving. "So wet, baby. I think you like this talk about me spanking you." His fingers slide inside me, and I pant, my hips lifting with his exploration, when I really want to grab him and push myself closer.

He's merciless in his exploration, stretching me, stroking me, and the only thing that allows me to maintain my control is the promise that he will soon be inside me. But I'm so close to the edge, so ready to come, that I moan with the ache of my body, but I hold onto the bed, afraid he'll stop, certain he'll deny me any moment.

He leans in and kisses me, and it all but undoes me. My arms need to be wrapped around his neck, and when his hand covers my breast and teases my nipple, I'm melting right here in this bedroom. My lashes lower, and I wish for something I can clench but there is only wood. My breasts are high, thrust into the air, and I want him to touch my nipples, lick them too, but he denies me what I want.

Instead, he leans in close, his cheek to mine, his fingers pulling out of me, to cup my sex, and he says, "Not yet."

My entire body screams in rejection, and my fingers curl in my palms, as it's all I can do not to capture his that rests on my waist. "You're trying to make me touch you," I whisper.

"Touch me, and I'll let you come," he promises.

"And then you'll spank me?" I challenge.

"You'll like it."

"I can make myself come."

He laughs low and soft and kisses me. "But we both know it's better when I do it for you." He catches me to him, and I touch him, there's just no way around it, before he turns me to face the post, and I'm forced to catch my hands on the hard surface, which should be him, but it's the post again.

The idea that he's about to spank me sends my pulse soaring. Adrenaline takes control and I try to turn around. Damion pins me between the post and his powerful thighs and hips, filling his hands with my breasts, exploring my waist, then my hips, and yes, then, my backside.

"Damion," I say urgently.

He squeezes my backside and murmurs, "I'd never spank you without permission, Alana. Trust me, baby." His teeth scrape my shoulder, and he says, "*Trust me.*" There's something about the way he repeats those words, and I know they run deeper than sex. They're about our history, about the love and hate, and push and pull, that is carved into our every moment together.

But his request is easier said than done, when the lifetime behind us still defines us far more than any lifetime before us, and the minute he steps away from me, I try to turn. He flattens his hand on my back. "*Trust me.*"

It's not a command, as one might expect in the circumstance, but rather a request, and that's what undoes me.

And the truth is I do trust him, with everything but my fragile heart. I know he won't spank me without my permission. I know he won't hurt me. And when he says he'll give me a dozen orgasms, he means to make that vow come true. I have nothing to lose, and I whisper, "I do."

He waits there a moment, his hand still on my lower back, as if he is giving me time to change my mind. I can almost feel him battling within himself over me and this moment, and I don't know why but his emotions and his arousal collide and crash over me. A moment later, his hand slides over my hip and backside and then falls away from my body, but my skin tingles where he touched me.

I'm vulnerable all over again.

He's good at doing that to me.

There's a shift in the air, and I know he's moved away, the sound of clothing rustling about, and I know now that he is naked, too.

# Chapter Twelve

I know he's behind me before he ever touches me. That's the thing about me with Damion. I feel him on some level that defies any reality I know with any other human being. I can't even explain what that means, but if he's close, *I know*. It's like a tingling sensation, an awareness that reaches beyond the conscious being.

And right now, he's so close I can feel the heat of his body, a moment later, the press of his cock to my hip. I swallow hard and hold my breath, waiting for what comes next. His hands settle on my waist, and his touch torments my nerve endings in the best of ways.

He leans in and draws in a breath as if he's inhaling my scent, "Turn around." There is this raw, achy need in the depths of his voice that radiates through me and has me twisting around to face him.

The minute I do, he's right in front of me, his sculpted, naked body intimately framing mine. His fingers tangle into my hair, his grip rough, erotic. "I'm not going to spank you," he says, "but, God, woman, I want to do every naughty thing you'll let me do to you."

I'm caught up in the moment, in the absolute intimacy between us right here and now, finally touching. "Do it," I whisper.

"You have no idea how much I could take from you if you let me, so don't let me. Not yet." He pauses, his lashes lowering, as he murmurs, "*Damn it*." And when he looks at me again, he says, "It's going to kill me when I lose you," before his mouth closes down over mine and he kisses me—no, he *consumes* me. This is not *just* a kiss at all. It's tenderness, demand, passion, torment, and *love,* and the mood of push and pull is gone.

I don't even try to tell him he doesn't have to lose me, it doesn't have to be that way. He's not in the right headspace right now, and maybe, I'm not either. Besides, I'm touching him now, as I've wanted to touch him for what feels like a lifetime. Touching him everywhere, anywhere I can, and I am not shy about it. I wrap one hand around his thick erection. He groans with the impact, and the power I've wielded over him is a high I can't explain. His hand grips mine over his erection as pumps into my grip, but grows quickly impatient.

He palms my backside and lifts me, my breasts molded to his chest, my legs wrapping his waist, and he walks to a large chair in the corner and sits down with me on top of him. I straddle him, his erection is between us, pressed to my belly, and the hunger we have for one another is dark and edgy. I can feel it cloaking us like a heavy blanket, pulling us together.

My hands land on his shoulders, and he catches a strand of my hair and twines it around his fingers, tugging lightly. "Come here."

That's the definition of power. To command me with a single strand of my own hair around his finger. It's so very hot. I'm hot. I'm melting right here, on top of him. I ease forward, closer to the man who destroys me with a word and touch, sensations swirling in my belly, my nipples tight. "You've always been bossy."

"And you've always loved to play with my toys."

I laugh, and I love that I can be naked and aroused and still laugh with Damion. "Nothing has changed, I guess—"

I barely get the words out and he's drinking me in again, kissing me with long, sensual strokes of his tongue before he murmurs, "I've needed to be inside you again for a lifetime it seems."

I wet my lips and say, "Yes. Please."

"Hmmm. I like that word—*please.* I'm going to make you say it again and often."

He catches my waist and anchors me, while I reach for his cock and guide his erection where we both need him to be, pushing him against me, past the slick heat of my sex. He is big and hard, and he presses into me, deep, then deeper, the look on his face pure male satisfaction. I pant and take all of him, sliding down the hard length of him, taking every inch of him, and it feels oh, so good.

*He* feels so good.

My hands are back on his impressive shoulders, and our gazes collide, and I can only describe what we share as raw hunger and emotion. And for a moment or ten, I have no idea, we just stare at each other, but all of our past is there with us, all that has been and might be in the future. It's complicated, and right as it is wrong. Because this little time out we're sharing has nothing to do with sex, and yet everything to do with why we want each other to the point of addiction.

He reaches up and teases my nipples, sensations rocking through my body, clenching my sex, and my fingers dive roughly into his hair.

I don't know how those small acts unleash the wild in us, but they do. Our hunger for one another erupts and suddenly we are kissing, swaying, touching each other. My body is hypersensitive to everything he does, and I have no reserve. I ride him, rock against him, while he kisses me, fucks me, and just plain drives me wild. I am so very close to orgasm, the best kind of orgasm, with him inside me. I want it. I press into reaching for it, but I also don't want this to end.

Somehow his mouth ends up on my nipple, sucking as I sway against him, and that's all she wrote. I gasp and hold onto him while my body stiffens and then shatters. It is the most intense orgasm of my life. Damion groans, wraps his arms around me, and pulls me against his cock with a hard thrust. And then he's right there with me, his face buried in my neck as his body quakes beneath mine.

We end with him collapsed on the chair and me collapsed on top of him, for I don't know how long, both of us breathing heavily. We just lay there, long moments passing, and I really don't want to leave this spot. Because when we do, when reality returns, we are one giant lifetime of goodbyes.

# Chapter Thirteen

"Let's go clean up, baby," Damion says softly, stroking my hair, and before I can respond, he's standing and taking me with him.

Suddenly, I'm thinking about him and his *it'll kill me when I lose you* statement, or whatever it was he said, but it told a story. He's already decided we are temporary. A few seconds later, he deposits me on the floor of his massive, sparkling master bathroom and hands me a towel. I accept his offering, and when he reaches for another, I make my escape. "I need to go to the bathroom," I declare, and dart around him and enter the stall, shutting the door and leaning against it.

I don't actually pee when I probably should—the whole after sex thing—but I clean up and sit on the edge of the toilet seat. What am I doing with Damion? Why can't I ever just walk away? *Because,* I think, *he gives me all the feels, and no one else ever has.* And because I've tasted his pain and felt it, too, and I don't really understand where it comes from but it makes me feel like he needs me.

A loud knock on the door has me jolting. "Alana?"

"Yes?" My voice trembles ridiculously in a telling way with that one single word.

"You okay in there?"

I stare down at the sparkling ring on my finger, a ring he really did pick for me, which means something. It might even mean a whole heck of a lot. I'd tried to take it off, but Damion had rejected the idea, and insisted I wear it. Because he wanted me to? Because he's afraid I'll walk away before he's ready. "I just need a minute, okay?"

"Can you take it with me?" he asks softly and there is a vulnerability in his voice I've rarely heard in our lifetime of knowing each other. My belly clenches as I remember that he only shows that softer side of himself to me, or at least, I think he does.

I run my hand through my hair and stand up, but I'm ridiculously nervous to open the door, and I really don't understand why. "Can you just give me a minute, please?"

"Please don't shut me out," he replies, and the plea that defies his cool control and confidence, is what does me in. It means something, just like the ring, and him wanting me to wear it does, too.

I open the door.

He's standing there in long slung sweatpants, his ridiculously perfect body stretched tall, his arm resting on the doorframe above my head, his gaze probing, as he searches my face, but not for long. He drags me close, folding me into his long, lean muscle, as he declares, "I love you, woman. You *have to know that*. You have to feel it."

I don't doubt this to be true. I've never doubted we love each other. There are few people who endure a lifetime of drifting apart and coming back together as we have, but—there are so many buts. I just don't really know where that love falls in a sea of possibilities. My fingers curl on his chest. "I love you, too. I always have. I always will. Also, I really need a shirt or something. Please? Because I can't be naked when you're not, not right now."

"I'd rather just take you back to bed."

"We were never in the bed."

"Let's fix that. We'll order take out and eat in bed. *Our bed*, Alana." He cups my face. "Come on, baby. Try out what it's like to live with me, at least for tonight and tomorrow morning."

"You do know that it's hard to get rid of someone who lives with you, right?"

"I don't want to get rid of you. Ever." He caresses my hair behind my ear in a tender act that sends shivers through me. "Never."

"And yet, you told me losing me would kill you."

"I'm done leaving. It's you who will leave. You want to leave now." His tone is one part accusation and one part something that feels like defeat when he is never defeated.

"I don't want to leave, Damion. I want you to stop pushing me away."

He catches my hand and gives me one of his heated inspections. "You're gorgeous, smart, compassionate, and a better person than I will ever be. I'd be a fool to push you away, Alana. I don't want another man to touch you or sleep with you ever again. Or make breakfast with you the morning after fucking you. Or anything else, for that matter. Let's order food and go to bed."

I'm a ball of confusion with Damion, I am, but there is something in him tonight. I try to hear what he's saying, what he's *really* saying, but it might take morning light and clothing to allow that to happen. I nod, and he cups my face and kisses me. "I know a taco place I think you'll love. You do love tacos."

It's a reminder of the familiar between us. "Tacos always sound good."

"Then go pee, since we both know you didn't. I'll order and"—he points at the walk-in closet in the back of the bathroom—"grab whatever you want to wear." He kisses me hard and fast and exits the bathroom, pulling the door shut behind him.

He's giving me the moment I'd asked for because Damion gets me. I really do need it, but it wouldn't have been good if I had it before he said all he just said. I walk into his closet, the spicy scent of him everywhere, wreaking havoc on my brain cells and body. I step to the center of the giant room, eyeing Damion's well-organized clothing, all the expensive suits lined on one wall, his causal wear on another, and yet there is a ton of space left over. Space in which I could easily imagine all my things mingled with his, and the idea sits in my belly, feeling like it's supposed to happen. I'm going to move in with him, the consequences be damned. I already know this, so why am I even fighting it?

I grab a shirt, pull it on, and then dig through a drawer to find a pair of his socks, suddenly eager to stop overthinking and get back to Damion. I go pee, clean up a bit, and even spray a little dollop of his cologne on, inhaling the delicious male scent. When I return to the bedroom, he's entering the room with a bottle of wine and two glasses in hand.

"Wine?" he asks.

I nod and he pours me a glass, both of us sitting down on the bed as he grabs the remote but pauses to nuzzle my neck. "Why do you smell like me?"

I laugh at that. "I'm pretty sure you're all over me."

"Yes, but that's not it." He eases back to look at me. "Did you put on my cologne?"

My cheeks heat and I confess, "I like it on you. I thought you might like it on me."

He strokes hair from my face and tilts my gaze to his. "I do." His voice is low and gravelly before he kisses me. "I'm so fucking glad you're here."

My chest tightens with emotion. "Me, too."

He kisses me and then releases me to flip on the TV, finding a specific channel he's hunting for, which turns out to be the Hallmark Channel. I laugh and shake my head. "I know you do not watch this."

"I actually do every once in a while, when I'm missing the old days. It reminds me of going to your house. You and your mom always had it on."

My heart squeezes with the idea that holds our past as close to his heart as I do. "We did," I agree, "but I won't subject you to watching it."

The doorbell rings, and he hands me the remote. "Leave it on Hallmark. I'll get the food."

"You think it's already here?"

"Oh yeah. The taco place is right next door." He pushes to his feet, and crosses toward the bedroom door, the flex of his back muscles holding my attention as he exits the room. Someone is getting an impressive show when he opens the door, because Damion is a specimen.

It's a long time later, when we really have finished a super cute Hallmark movie, and our bellies are full of amazing tacos. Damion turns off the TV and rolls us to our sides, facing each other, our legs curled together, his hands on my hips. "You know that song that was on when we were downstairs. It's by Masked Wolf—"

"Astronaut in the Ocean."

"Yeah, that one. It reminds me of you."

"Me?" I ask, surprised, though it's not an unfamiliar feeling, even when it played tonight. "Why?"

"You've always been the astronaut, destined to soar higher and higher, while the rest of us try to pull you into an ocean of sharks."

I'm stunned by this comparison, and I am certain it confirms what I've read in him. He's afraid of pulling me under and drowning me.

"When I say I have to protect you," he adds, "it's not out of obligation. It's out of my personal need to take care of you. I just keep getting it wrong."

"I'm here now," I say, emotion welling in my belly. "If you don't let go, you didn't get it wrong this time."

He nods and pulls back the covers. We climb under, and he reaches over and turns out the light. Damion pulls me down on the bed, folding me close, holding me almost a little too tight as he says, "I don't want to get it wrong with you, Alana."

But he thinks he will.

That's the unspoken message but I also realize that he's told me I'm an astronaut and he's a shark in the ocean. I think—I think he's our worst enemy, and maybe his own, too, and it's time for him to see himself through my eyes. It's time for me to hold onto him as hard as he's holding onto me right now. Even if that means I stand toe to toe with his father in a proverbial war. I think of my mother crying about that man forcing her to have sex with him. I've let that go. Why have I let that go?

This is war, and Damion's father is my enemy, and his as well.

And the best place to fight it is by Damion's side.

# Part Two

"Hell hath no fury like a woman scorned"

—William Congreve's play, The Mourning Bride (1697).

And before this is over, Alana will be that woman...

# Chapter Fourteen

## Damion

> "In every woman there is a Queen. Speak to the Queen and the Queen will answer."
>
> — Norwegian Proverb.

I wake to a room cloaked in darkness, with my cellphone incessantly ringing and Alana's soft, naked body tucked in front of mine, with me wrapped around her. I'm not even thinking about answering that call. I savor the impossibility of finally having her here with me, finally holding her, fucking her, just being with her. Alana is in my bed, where she belongs. I nuzzle her neck, addicted to the sweet floral scent of her and the warmth of her next to me. She snuggles her sweet little backside against my thickening erection and murmurs my name, reaching behind her to rasp her fingers over the stubble on my jaw. My hand slides over the silk of her skin and I cup her breast, and thank fuck, my phone goes silent.

"Your phone," she murmurs, as if it's only now registered in her mind. "It's dark. What if it's important?"

As if she's willed it to life, the damn thing starts to ring again.

"Holy hell," I grind out and brush my mouth over hers. "You know this has to do with my father's bullshit games."

"You have to take it," she urges, and I know she's right. "I'll be here when you're done."

I relinquish my hold on Alana and roll for my phone, my damn cock hard enough at this point to hammer the asshole calling me to death. Snatching my cell from the nightstand, I note the six am hour and the caller ID. It's officially confirmed. This is bullshit calling. I flip on the nightstand light, sit up, and answer, "Let me guess, Max. You've talked to my father." Max being the most influential member of the board.

"Not me," he says, "but he's talking in a lot of ears and putting me in a crap position. I want to move the board meeting. They all do."

"That's bullshit." I throw the blanket away and settle my feet on the ground. "This is done. They all signed commitments. Legally binding commitments."

"And we all want to keep those deals—"

"Contractual obligations," I correct.

He clears his throat. "There's a problem, son. Your father has 'something' on everyone, and he's made threats. We all need time to get our houses in order. If we vote today, the board will risk your wrath over his, and your father wins."

"He won't win when I sue."

"And you'll plunge our stock to the deep, dark depths of hell."

"We'll recover, and I'll build a board that isn't filled with a bunch of crooks."

"Let's meet. Give me until late afternoon. Let's have drinks. I'll text you."

Agitation has me pushing to my feet. "Let me be clear with you, Max. There are other ways I can handle this, but none of them are as lucrative for you as this option. Make it happen. And fuck drinks. In or out. If you're out, I know what to do."

He's silent a beat. "I'll make it happen. Give me the week."

"You have until Monday."

"It's Friday."

"Monday it is."

"Tuesday," he counters.

"*Monday.*" I hang up.

"Damion?"

Alana's voice is a blast of sweetness, honey in the hard whiskey bite of my father's bullshit. She's finally here, by my side, in my bed, and I cannot even say I'm selfish for pulling her into this anymore. All those years apart did nothing to protect her. The reality is, she's been marked by my family from the moment her family moved in next to mine. I'm sure my father thought she'd be a coming-of-age fuck buddy, and I'd soon move on to a more suitable match in his eyes. But she was, and is, so much more to me—my best friend, a fantasy, a moral compass when my father taught me to have nothing but a pitchfork and a bullet for my enemies.

I hate what I became without her and how tempted I am to bring that part of me out to play, to end this with my father and protect Alana. But I never want her to see that part of me. I will *never* let her see that part of me.

"Damion," she says again, and I shake myself out of my reverie and turn to face her.

I swear, just seeing her there in my bed—*our bed,* if I get my way—her hair all mussed up and sexy, is as surreal as it gets. And when she snatches up my shirt from the end of the bed and pulls it over her, offering me a flash of a pretty pink nipple, I'm rock hard all over again. Her in my shirt says she's mine.

"Morning, baby," I greet.

"But not a good one, right?" She shifts to her knees. "What's happening?"

"What we already know is happening. My father climbed into everyone's heads and started turning their minds to mush. I need to shower and go into work." I toss my phone on the bed and offer her my hand. "Come shower with me."

She scoots closer and presses her hand to mine. "That's not the way to get ready quickly."

"It's in everyone's best interest that I fuck you before I go to work and fuck them."

She doesn't laugh, and neither do I. She climbs out of the bed and says, "Let's go shower."

A few minutes later, hot water streams over our naked bodies, and the sweet little girl next door is on her knees with my cock in her hand. Holy fuck, she'll be the death of me. The way she sucks me deep and licks me everywhere just reinforces that she's my dream girl. She always was, and she sure as fuck is this morning. When it's over and she's sucked me dry, swallowed, and done every naughty thing the boy next door dreamed of her doing for almost all my life, the edge of my mood is decidedly tamped down, and she's wrapping her arms around me. "Feel better?"

"If you're trying to convince me you shouldn't live with me, that's not the way to do it."

She smiles and says, "I can't move until my season is done filming in two weeks, but I can bring some things over if you can help me."

I go still, not sure I've heard her right. "Did you just say yes?"

"I'm pretty sure I did that last night. You do know that once I move in, it's hard to get rid of me."

"Make no mistake, baby. I'm keeping you this time."

"Unless you decide leaving protects me."

I open my mouth to make my case, but she presses her fingers to my lips. "I don't want to hear whatever you're going to say. I made my decision. You'll probably hurt me. I know this, but good, bad, or ugly, I'm moving in with you."

I catch her hand, hating with a passion that she believes that's how this goes, that's how this ends. "I never wanted to hurt you, but the truth is, I wasn't the man you needed me to be then, but I am now. Only good this time. I'm going to make it happen."

"I don't want you to promise it's all good because we both know that's not real life or reality. I just want you to face the bad with me this time. I can handle it."

I pull her under the water with me and hold her close, but I don't say anything because I can't. Because she's too good to understand how bad bad can get. And how dark I am, even if I don't want to be anymore. But I might have to be that man one more time.

To protect her. To protect a lot of people.

# Chapter Fifteen

Despite Alana's objections, I arrange a private car for her personal use starting with her ride to work this morning. "That's not necessary," she argues, her nipples puckering beneath the silk of her robe, her long, wet hair draping her delicate shoulders.

"It is necessary. You're a star now. There will undoubtedly be a few out-of-control fans which requires proper precautions to ensure your safety," I tighten the strings on her robe to close the gap before we both end up naked again. "I'll see you soon and talk to you sooner."

She pushes to her toes and wraps her arms around my neck, a smile on her sexy little mouth. "I like this new reality where the words 'I see you soon' means hours not years."

My hand slides up over her back, molding her close, the warmth of her body seeping through my palms. "Me too, baby," I say, my voice softening with the words. "Me too. It's long past due." I catch a strand of her hair in my fingers. "And I like how wet you are all the time."

She laughs. "The wrong kind of wet."

"I'll fix that later," I promise, kissing her firmly on the mouth. "I'll update you later. I'll lock up as I leave." I set her away from me and exit the bathroom, but I can feel her eyes on me as I cross the living room. At the door, I turn back and wink at her before I exit to the hallway, pausing for just a moment to savor how damn good it feels to have Alana in my life. And how right it feels to have her in my apartment, and my personal space. It's as if every other woman was a visitor and she's come home.

To me.

Where she always belonged.

Five minutes later, I'm in the rear of a hired SUV, where I arrange the car service for Alana and text her the details. My driver is headed toward Alexander's office, Alexander being a close friend and my attorney. He's also the attorney who created that binding agreement the stockholders signed, and he's apparently being bombarded with calls over it this morning. I myself have had four calls from board members, and per Alexander's guidance, I've declined them all when I'd prefer to answer and tell them to fuck off. The agreements are signed. Unlike my father, I don't play games. If they back out of their contractual obligation, I'll sue them. They now have to decide if they prefer that public and financial disgrace to whatever my father has promised to bring upon them. If they're all stupid enough to sign on with me when they're indebted to him, effectively splitting their loyalties, then they're the wrong people for the board anyway, and losing them will be a win.

I'm solid. I've covered my ass. They won't talk me into letting them out of the agreement.

If Alexander prefers to deliver the pain, I'll give him that gift.

The one text that has my attention is my father's "fixer," Caleb, which reads short and simple: *Call me.*

I don't know if it's the ex-CIA agent in him that makes him a man of few words or if he was just born that way, but it's the only way to work for my father, which he still does, way too often. But Caleb is loyal to only a paycheck, and maybe me. *Maybe.* He's the reason I knew Alana's father had foolishly set his sights on my father and was about to end up dead. But I've also told him to back off and get out before I destroy my father, and him with him, but I'm not sure a man who loves money as much as Caleb does can help but play both sides of a large bill.

Either way, my priorities are in order. Caleb has to wait. My first phone call is to my assistant Naomi, who used to be my mother's assistant, which makes her loyal to me and disloyal to my father, which is exactly how I like it. "Damion," she greets. "How did your meeting go last night?"

"My father showed up."

"Oh crap. How bad?"

Crap is her version of fuck, and she doesn't approve of my version, which is just plain fuck. "Pain in the ass bad, but—"

"You expected him."

"I expected something." I shift the topic to the point of the call. "I need to arrange a mover to pick up Alana's things as soon as she's done filming her season. They can pack for her, too."

"Forgive me if I don't understand the words coming out of your mouth. Alana, as in the TV star you grew up with and your mother always believed you were in love with."

"Yes. Her."

"Does your mother know?"

"She will when we hang up and you call her."

She doesn't laugh. "Yes, but it should really come from you."

"I can't with my mother right now, so feel free to steal that thunder."

"She'll call you," she warns, because her own mothering tendencies can't be tamed, even if it means she's protecting me from my own mother.

"Right," I say dryly. "Tell her after the board meeting happens, which is now next Monday."

"Why? I thought it was today?"

"I'll explain later. I need to go. I'll be in mid-morning if anyone is looking for me."

"Three of the board members already came hunting."

"They can wait in hell while burning to death, as far as I'm concerned."

"Got it. Blow them off. Check. What else?"

"Nothing." My phone starts buzzing, and I glance at caller ID to find Caleb calling, his urgency setting off alarms. "I have a call coming in I need to take. Talk later." I flip to Caleb and answer with, "I've never known you to be impatient."

"I just watched your father pick Alana's mother up at her apartment."

A cold, hollow feeling settles in my gut. This is going nowhere good, and Alana is going to be the one who gets hurt. "Then it's not over."

"No, it's not over. Now ask me why I was at her parent's apartment in the first place."

*Holy hell*, I think. "Do I want to know?"

"He has me following her father again."

"Did that ever end?"

"For me it did, though I know for a fact he had cheaper eyes on him. But he has me now, and I'm expensive."

My fingers thrum on my knee. "Any idea why?"

"You're fucking with him. And don't think for a minute you're immune to his evil because you're his son."

I give a humorless laugh. "You do know who you're talking to, right?"

"It's easy to forget when he's in this close proximity. He won't come at you directly. He'll come at what you love. And that means Alana."

My fingers go still and then curl into my palm. "I'm aware. I'm keeping her close."

"Get her protection. You've been warned." He disconnects.

# Chapter Sixteen

I arrive at the Starbucks next door to Alexander's office, where we've agreed to meet in the next fifteen minutes. With time to kill, I order a drink and settle at a private corner table, with Caleb's warning screaming on repeat in my head. It doesn't matter what his intent is with that phone call; it requires action. I'm instantly thinking of a guy who did some tech work for me in Europe and who I both respect and actually like—a combination I don't come by easily. Blake Walker is not only sought after by government and private sectors for his world-class hacking skills; he and his two older brothers own Walker Security, one of the most well-respected, full-service security firms across the globe. I don't know his brothers, but I know him, and he's one of the few men I'd pit against Caleb and give him a shot at winning.

For just a moment, I'm back in the shower with Alana this morning, hot water streaming around us, me holding her sexy body against mine, and I tell myself I'm a changed man, worthy of her in every way. The past doesn't matter. She doesn't have to know everything. I shake off the memory and focus on what has always mattered the most: protecting her. And the days when I do that by stepping away are over.

I snap up my phone from the table where I set it, scroll past several desperate and/or demanding text messages from board members, and tab through my phonebook. Once I've located Blake's number, I punch the autodial, and he answers on the first ring. "Damion, my man," he greets. "I see you're back in the States and New York. How the fuck are you?"

Blake uses the word "fuck" like a sentence connector and somehow makes it likable. Maybe because I like the word "fuck" as well, especially where Alana is concerned. "Should I ask how you know I'm in the States?" I ask.

"The real question is, why would you be calling to hire me if I didn't know? Who the fuck would want that dumbass. That *is* why you're calling me, right? To hire me?"

I sip my coffee, set my phone down, open my earbuds, and stick one in my right ear before I say, "Let's talk Alana Blue, who's become a local celebrity."

"I know who she is, and she's more than a local celebrity. That little show of hers is all kinds of viral. My wife watches it all the damn time. Hell, a couple of my guys watch it. Who is she to you?"

"I could tell you I'm on the board that got her that show, which would be true."

"But not the whole story. She matters to you."

"Very much. We've known each other since we were kids, but things were complicated."

"The best things in life are, man. What's got you on the phone with me? Some sort of stalker situation?"

I laugh without humor and glance around, ensuring there are no nearby ears. "Somehow calling my father a stalker is ridiculously accurate."

"Your father? What kind of shit show are you in right now?"

"Yeah, I'm just going to shoot straight. He wants the company to strive on destroying others. I do not, and I'm influencing the board to find a better way. I've crossed my father. He will take revenge, and that means Alana."

"Would your father really go after your woman?"

"Our families lived next door for years. There's personal history there and a whole lot of baggage. He always felt they were beneath us and that Alana was a distraction."

"A familiar story."

"Until I tell you my father's fucking her mother, which is supposedly her way of paying off money Alana's father borrowed from my father to pay off a gambling debt. Then Alana's father found out they were sleeping together and tried to dig up dirt on my father to turn in to the police. That's why I came home. To protect Alana and her family."

"So, you really think he'd go after your woman?"

"I know he would."

"All right then. Noted. And for the record, it's not as crazy a story as you might think–I've heard a lot of crazy—but it's one ripe for something rotten."

"Which is why I stayed away from Alana. I thought she'd grow up, move away, and be happy. But our families didn't let that happen, and at this point, I'm done walking away from her. She's with me. She's moving in with me. It's time to defuse the threat."

"There are a lot of ways I might be able to help with that," he says. "For instance, giving your father a reason to stand down, and that can be done in a great many ways. But first things first, we need to get protection in place for Alana and her family. I can get a man on Alana this afternoon, but it's going to be next week before I can support her parents."

"As long as Alana's protected."

"I have a guy who just got back to the States I have in mind. This is well-timed for him. He needs a break—not that this job is easy—but compared to what he just came off, it's a walk in the park."

"Which was what?"

"Extracted a hostage from a hostile, at great peril to himself. The hostage is safe."

"And who's dead?" I ask, wanting to know more about the man who will protect the woman I love.

"Who the fuck do you think is dead?" Blake asks. "The bad guys. Adam's one of the good guys, Damion. He's former SEAL Team Six and, as a bonus, master of disguises. I'm telling you, this man is a giant, and he can still disappear anywhere. It's totally fucking nuts."

I'm reasonably comforted, though on edge, where Alana is concerned, for about ten thousand and one reasons, those reasons ranging from her safety to all the ways I could lose her. "He's going to need those skills and more," I say, forcing my focus on what I can change, which is how Alana's protected, not what I can't change in my past. "There's a guy on my father's payroll. Caleb Ross. He's a former CIA agent, and I believe he'd kill for the right payday and probably has. He and I get along, and he's shown signs of a conscience, but I don't know that he's truly loyal to anyone or anything that is not his bank account."

"What's making you bring him up right now?"

"He warned me my father is fucking Alana's mother again—"

"Again?" he interrupts.

"I thought it had ended, and Alana's mother claimed it had, but obviously it has not. I'm not sure she doesn't want to be with Alana's father. Maybe they were together when we were growing up. I don't know the real picture."

"I'll find out," he assures me. "But go on."

"At one point, Caleb was following Alana's father on alert to act if necessary, and no, I don't know what that means, but I can guess. He was pulled off, and the heat seemed to shift. Now, he's back on."

"Did he give you details?"

"He told me to protect Alana and her family, but he's the kind of guy who'd tell me that and then take the job to end them."

There's pounding on his keyboard before he says, "His file's classified, but I can get to it. We'll handle him. I'll have Rick Savage join Adam next week. He's an ex-mercenary and he'll do what needs to be done."

"And Adam won't?"

"Adam will force Savage to think twice before he acts, and if Savage still wants to do it, he'll help him. Caleb will never survive him, let alone him and Adam together. What else do I need to know?"

My lips press together, and I admit what I have never said out loud, "My father doesn't mind taking a life if it makes his better."

Blake's response is instant and unphased. "Do you have the ammunition to check him?"

"Some. Not enough."

"We better get some. I'm buried in work, but I'll make time for you. Let me do some deep dives and come up with something."

"When can you get Adam on Alana?"

"Three hours."

*Not a minute too soon*, I think, and continue the call long enough to get Blake everything he needs to get Adam to me, and most importantly, to protecting Alana. We disconnect right as Alexander enters the coffee shop.

I have Alana back in my life. I'm not losing her. And I'm damn sure not allowing my father to take her from me. I'll do whatever it takes to protect her and make him go away. Forever.

# Chapter Seventeen

Alexander is tall, fit, and well dressed in only the most expensive of suits he earned by excelling at about everything he does. We met in college, where he managed to be both a player with the women and a top performer in his classes. We became friends, and I can say he's one of the only people who got me back then and still gets me now because we're alike. We're focused, driven, and on a path to become our fathers' protégés.

Neither of us did. His owns a massive electronics company and manages his business about like my father, which is why Alexander is now one of the most sought-after corporate attorneys in the country, rather than his father's protégé.

I lift my hand and catch his eye, and he walks my direction, his strides long and heavy, his expression grim. Something's happened, and that something is, no doubt, *my father*. He settles in front of me, a tic in his jaw.

"What'd he do?"

"He showed up at my office with Alana's mother on his arm."

My chin lowers and I sigh. "Damn it to hell," I say, reaching for my cup. "Can I have some bourbon for this coffee? To what end?"

"Content-wise, the conversation was a bunch of lame threats, and he was aware there was no substance to them. My read was the conversation wasn't the point. Alana's mother was. He was sending you a message. Knowing your history with Alana, and your father, I don't like where that's leading me."

*Nor do I*, I think, because the message is crystal clear.

He's telling me that he's close to Alana, he can get to her at any time, and I better not forget it. If I ruin him, he will ruin me, and start with Alana. If I take everything from him, he has nothing to lose. I have everything to lose. He'll expose all my secrets and dirty laundry, even if it's his own.

I knew this was coming, of course. I'm hyperaware of the immediate need to come clean with Alana, but I need time, and my father's ripped that from my hands. I knew this could happen, of course, but not under these dire circumstances. We need a foundation of commitment between us first, one that I haven't fully created despite how fucking much I want her in my life, and forever this time.

In a perfect world, this wouldn't happen now. It would happen after time has passed, after she's lived with me, and I've reminded her that I'm still the person she knows like no one else knows me. It would be after I told her that she's always been my lighthouse, guiding me through stormy waters, from darkness to light.

Only then would I tell her there was a time when I allowed myself to be sucked under and into the waves. A time when she felt so far away that there was no reason not to allow the current to claim me.

She can't be my lighthouse if she's pulled into treacherous water with me.

Protect her first, I silently vow. Marry her later.

If she'll even have me when my father is done with me.

# Chapter Eighteen

## *Alana*

I arrive at the studio in the hired car Damion insisted become my regular means of transportation. I'd wanted to refuse such a luxury, but when I'd tried, Damion's determination was clear. He didn't do this just for me. He did it because he was worried about me, and I don't remember the last time anyone worried about me at all. Except him.

I burst through the studio doors in a mad rush, late to set for the first time since the show started. I'm dressed in jeans and sneakers and still riding the high of deciding to move in with Damion. This is where we've always been headed, and I can't say if it means we fly or sink, but we're at least finding out. I think, even if it goes south, for the first time in my life, I'll be at peace and able to move on. We never had closure between us, and now we're an open book full of possibilities, and at least the story can be written, be it with a happy or sad ending.

But my personal life needs to slide to the backseat for the moment.

I make a beeline for makeup, where I'll be prettied up, and then sent to wardrobe. I'm still amazed by the studio's desire to dress me in ridiculously expensive brands and then gift the outfits to me. Of course, I have to claim the items on my taxes, but it's a small price to pay for the best wardrobe of my life. *It's something for me*, I think, something my parents can't take from me, as they do every extra dime I earn. I can't go on like this, especially under Damion's looking glass.

I've become an enabler, I acknowledge once again, but I've done it so long that I probably need therapy to figure out why and how to stop. Or I need Damion to talk sense into me, not become my father's bank account, which is my biggest fear. I won't let that happen, I vow.

I enter the makeup studio to find Cheryl, my stylist, waiting on me with a Starbucks cup as an offering. "I know how to start your day right," she says, a smile on her lips, her brunette hair pinned atop her head with a few wayward strands poking out here and there. She's pretty and sweet, and everything I could wish for in someone who I work with almost daily.

"You're a goddess," I say, indicating my bag in hand. "Let me go put this away and I'll be right back."

"Hurry," she says, pointing to the clock on the wall. "We're late."

*I'm* late, she means, but she's too sweet to say as much, while my producer will not be so kind. The idea hurries my pace down a long hallway, the memory of Damion kissing me at the apartment door humming through me in all the right ways. He'd winked at me and exited the apartment, leaving me with hope in my heart that we're going to make this work.

Entering my dressing room, I'm greeted by a deliciously floral scent, shutting the door behind me and searching for the source of the sweet smell, only to light up at the sight of a giant double bouquet of roses sitting on my dressing table. My heart squeezes at the sweet act, and I'm even a little teary-eyed. Really, truly, having this man back in my life, and as my partner for the first time ever, is everything I ever wanted. He did this despite how stressed he is about the board meeting, which makes the gift unexpected and, oh, so sweet. I reach for my phone to call him, but I really am late, and on a film set, your time is not your own. Every second you're not where you're supposed to be costs the studio money.

I cross the room, toss my purse onto the chair, and then lean over the bouquet to inhale a single rose blossom, savoring the gift for just a moment. My gaze drops to the ring on my finger and as much as I don't want to take it off, the many ways it will get attention on set that I do not want to answer, are far too many. I seal it inside my purse while the note attached to the flowers goes inside my pants pocket where I ensure no one else reads it.

A few minutes later, I'm sitting in front of the mirror as Cheryl works her magic while I sip my coffee, dying to know what is in the message.

I'm about to sneak a peek when I hear, "What the holy heck is going on?"

At the sound of my producer's voice, the idea that I'm later than I think I am sets my heart racing. Cheryl's eyes meet mine in the mirror, hers wide with worry, which only makes *me* worry all the more. As if burned, her hands fall from my hair, and she backs away. That's my cue to twist my chair around, only to find Shauna standing right in front of me and shoving her phone in my direction. "What is this?"

I'd be happy to make a go at an answer if her phone wasn't literally, at this point, right in my face. She pulls it back and repeats, "*What is this*, Alana?"

*Now* I spy the screen, and considering it holds a picture of Damion kissing me outside the restaurant last night, his possessive hand resting on my lower back, I'd prefer to go back home and start the day over. If given the chance for that do-over, Damion and I could actually talk about the "what ifs" of what's happening right now.

"Are you sleeping with the boss?" she demands.

*Yes*, I think, *and loving every minute of it*, but I'm also aware that admitting any such thing creates the impression that I've spread my legs for my show. Which bites, and bites hard. I settle on a benign truth. "Damion and I grew up together."

"That's not an answer," she replies. "And I can see the doe in the headlights look on your face. I know he didn't get you the show. Even if Damion helped put you on the studio's radar, every studio exec could shove someone at us, and fail. You didn't fail. And a whole lot of people, including me, fell in love with your screenings and knew you wouldn't. The ratings are massive. But if you piss him off—"

I wave that idea off. "That's not going to happen."

"Says everyone who dates someone and thinks it can never go south."

"He was literally the first boy I ever kissed, and that was when we were seven years old. We grew up together. He knows me better than anyone in this world and I know him just as well. So *no*, he won't lash out at me, no matter what. And I won't lash out at him. We're *friends*, the kind that are few and far between. If we stop seeing each other, we will still be there for each other."

Her hands settle on her hips. "You grew up next door to him?"

"Yes. Yes, I did. I'm not endangering the show or anyone's job."

She grabs a chair and pulls it close, climbing in, and then studying me. "This is all over the press. We have to address it on the show."

My hands are up instantly. "No," I say firmly. "We will not. Damion's a private person and I will not go there."

"This is a reality show, and we can't ignore your reality when it's all over the press," she argues.

"Stop saying it's all over the press." I hold up a finger. "It's one photo."

"There will be more."

"So let people watch the show and hope we address it," I counter, "but we aren't going to talk about it. I won't. I'll walk off the show before that happens."

"Because he doesn't want you to talk about him? Have you asked him?"

"No. I have not. I know Damion—"

"*Ask him.* He knows what you do for a living. You need to ask, not assume. And you have a contractual obligation to deal with your personal life on camera. I'll give you time to talk to Damion, but the studio has pressured me to get more personal with you. We can start with your parents, if you prefer, and whatever squabbles there are between you–and don't tell me there are none. I saw you fighting with your father the other day."

"I'm not—"

"You are. You have to give me something. If you prefer, we can have you join a dating site. Maybe Damion would prefer that to himself being exposed?" She doesn't wait for an answer. She eyes her watch and taps it. "We're late." She motions to Cheryl. "Why aren't you finishing her hair?" She snaps her fingers. "Get her into wardrobe." She stands up and walks toward the door, and I stare after her as she disappears into the hallway.

Why would she push this hard for such a thing when Damion's her boss? Unless his spot on the board doesn't actually give him that power? I reject that idea the minute it pops in my head. No. That's wrong. Damion *has* the power, which means nothing about what just happened adds up. There's something off, something I'm not understanding.

Cheryl's gentle hand settles on my shoulder. "You okay?"

"Yes." I rotate around to face her. "I'm fine. Thank you."

"Don't let her get to you," she whispers. "And don't let her ruin a good thing between you and Damion."

*I think we're pretty good at that ourselves*, I think, but all I say is, "Thank you. I won't."

She smiles her approval. "Let's get you ready for the camera."

I nod and rotate to the mirror, and once Cheryl is fiddling with my hair again, I glance at the card in my hand, but I don't open it. At that point, I decisively slide it into my front jeans pocket. This place suddenly feels like a living, breathing creature that is as dangerous as it is intrusive. I'd much prefer to read the note later, when I'm alone, when it's just about me and Damion, not ratings.

# Chapter Nineteen

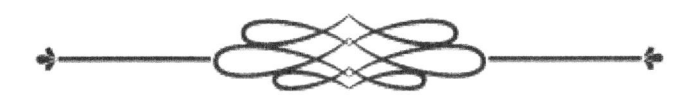

## *Damion*

I step off the elevator on the twenty-fifth floor of the West Building, and my gaze locks on the crown on the wall in the center of the West name. The arrogant prick that is my father really sees himself as a king, and therefore the ruling class, and therefore what he wishes to take, he will take.

In his mind, it's his right.

Just as it's my right as the younger generation to take his crown and send him into retirement.

I grit my teeth and cut right toward the lobby, pushing past the glass doors and into the reception area. A grand, bult-in desk with some sort of fucked-up wave-like design sits center stage. Debbie, my father's receptionist of five years, sits behind that ridiculous designer desk, her red hair pinned in an extreme bun.

"Good morning, Damion," she says, greeting me by my first name, as I prefer, while my father is Mr. West to her and everyone else; his name always spoken with a hint of fear.

Just how he likes it.

"Morning, Debbie," I greet. "Is my father in?"

Her spine stiffens and she bristles. "Yes, he is."

"That good of a mood, huh?"

"He's about average as far as I can see."

In other words, he's always a jerk to her and everyone who works for him. No surprise there. Literally, this entire floor is about catering to him and his moods. Here is where he has a dedicated staff, a fully stocked bar, a gym, a spa, and a personal chef who serves only him, all of which he pays for by destroying other people. What excited me as a young buck is now disgusting to me as a grown man. But it's true that I wanted to be like him.

Just like him.

That's the me I do not want Alana to ever know.

"I'm afraid I'm about to make it worse, Debbie," I warn, "so take cover."

Her face pinches with dread. "Do you have to?"

"We'll all be better for it," I promise, after which I round her desk and enter the hallway that leads toward my father's office. There are consequences to his actions, and he is no longer immune, nor will he ever be again. So yes, I will be king one day, and sooner than he thinks, or this company will cease to exist.

It's the only way this can end.

Making the past right is the only way I stand any chance of her allowing me to wake up next to her every day for the rest of my life. Protecting her is no longer about sheltering her; it's about arming her with the truth. My father made sure of that the day he first slept with her mother and set the future in play.

So yes, hell will come calling in the process of his dethroning, and it will be brutal, but when it's over, as I just told Debbie, it will be for the better, and not for a few, but for many. Not sunshine and rainbows, but better.

I enter the alcove that is the exterior of my father's office, and I'm not surprised to find the secretary desk outside his office empty. He can't keep the seat filled, firing them all for doing nothing more than breathing. No wonder he has to have a mistress that's well-bribed and on her knees for him. *Like Alana's mother*, I think bitterly. I hope like hell I'm wrong, but a part of me isn't so sure her mother is as innocent as she seems, and that coming to light would destroy Alana.

I walk toward his office, and the desk plate on the secretary desk reads, *Ester*, who'd lasted a year, I hear. It was a miracle. Then one day she got the flu and wasn't in the right spot at the right time when he needed her. He axed her the way he wishes he could axe me, but that ship sailed a long time ago.

Without a knock, I open my father's office door and enter the room to find my father sitting behind his ridiculously large mahogany desk with his equally ridiculous giant wingback king's chair. The dark-haired man sitting across from him twists around at my entry to reveal himself as Max, the dirty bastard himself. My father's been talking in ears, all right. He meant *his* ear. Max pops to his feet.

"Damion," he greets, and he says my name like I'm a ghost here to haunt him.

He better bet his ass I am.

"What'd he promise you, Max?" I ask, closing the space between me and the desk and halting really damn close to Max.

"Get out, Damion," my father snaps, but the anger in his voice is feigned, the amusement in his eyes deep. He knew I'd come here this morning. He also wanted me to see Max with him—Max, who played into his hand like a puppy dog who panted his way to his office at his beck and call. I'd like to say I love my father because he's my father, but that is another ship that has long ago sailed.

He's headed to hell, he's not dragging me with him.

I was twenty-five when I'd finally seen that he wasn't just bad. He was evil. I even know the date. November 11$^{th}$.

I reach inside my jacket and pull out an envelope, tossing it on my father's desk, the contents of which detail every insider trade he's done since he was old enough to pee outside a diaper, though he may need one now. It was a gift from Blake that he miraculously produced in a few hours. "You go after anyone who votes with me, I'll release that to the press."

My father ignores my offering, his lips twitching. "Whatever you have in there, I have ten things better."

A bluff, considering every single one of those things he mentions exposes him as well, but he wants Max to think otherwise. One side of my mouth quirks. "Bring it." I stare him down and slowly shift my gaze to Max. "You're choosing the wrong side."

His spine stiffens. "I didn't choose a side at all. He called me to negotiate the terms of the board meeting."

"You mean how much of a payday you get for turning the votes? Tell them all the game is over." My attention shifts back to my father. "Let me know when you're ready to negotiate the terms."

"Terms?" he asks, one gray brow shooting up. "What terms?"

Now my lips quirk. "I think you can guess," I say, because we both know his biggest fear. And that fear is my mother's stock and what she decides to do with it. For years, she has enjoyed the money associated with owning it, but more so, how it made my father squirm. And yes, she's married to a billionaire, but it makes her feel like she was equal to him. But with time and age, she's left my father in the past and is now secure in her relationship with a man who doesn't treat her like less than him, as my father did.

She'll hand over her stock to me the minute I say *now*. The only reason I haven't given that word as of yet is that it will equate to a hostile takeover, which is exactly what I'm trying to convince the board is bad business.

My father's lips tighten, and his blue eyes sharpen like ice despite the fires of hell in their depths. "Never underestimate the king, my boy. I've been winning long before you started losing way too often."

"You lose a whole lot more than the board knows. But *I know,* and that's a problem for you, and them, if they stay by your side." My gaze sideswipes Max with that message meant for him. "Red or black. Old or new. Choose wisely." I rotate on my heels and walk toward the door.

It would appear to most I've won. Even me, if I wasn't my father's son. If I hadn't seen what a caged man will do, it's never pretty. And my father is a caged man. There's an attack coming, and it's going to be aimed at Alana. I need to prepare myself and her for what comes next.

# Chapter Twenty

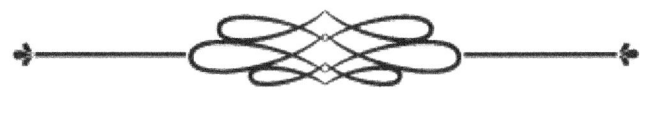

## *Alana*

The film set is an exact replica of the Blue Real Estate offices, which allows my parents to continue to operate their business while we film, at least a portion of the time. There are situations where we actually take over the offices for the full office effect, but those days are never as productive as those on set.

In a mere few hours, I film three client interviews, each of which will have their own episodes, and I'm now on number four. Which means four outfit changes. It's an exhausting process, but still fun. I might not have ever thought I wanted to be a TV star, and still don't love the spotlight, but my job is fun. Yes, there are reshoots, and retakes, and criticism, and I feel the pressure at times, but I'm blessed to do what I do for a living. My professional life is in order. It's my personal life where I face challenges. A point driven home by the fact that I'm in the middle of the last interview before lunch when the assistant producer, Lana–yes, we joke about how much our names sound alike—interrupts the shoot.

"Alana, you have an urgent phone call," she announces across the room.

At this point, I'm at a glass conference table, sitting across from an heir to a banking empire, Dierk Montgomery. To interrupt him when it was an act of God to get him to agree to the show—he only did it because his mother loves me—is not a smart idea. We need him back to film the rest of the segment. And for me, an urgent call most likely translates to a problem with my father.

I push to my feet, the teal blue designer dress I'm wearing falling just above my knees. "What's wrong?" I ask as Lana, a tall brunette, halts in front of me. "What's happening?" My voice is low, urgent.

"You just need to take this." She shoves the phone at me.

Nervously, my hand trembles, and the entire crew is watching me. "Hello."

"Alana."

At the sound of Damion's voice, I'm not sure if I should be even more scared to hear what's going on or angry at him for doing this to me. "What are you doing?" I ask, turning away from the piercing attention of the room and offering them my back.

"Hi, beautiful. Stop panicking, and don't be angry. I know what you're thinking, but you were going to get this call now from someone. I wanted it to be me."

"What is it?" I whisper urgently.

"You've got an extra season renewal, baby. And the only reason they didn't give you two seasons is that your contract is up for negotiation, which means it's time to get a raise."

Excitement and disbelief light me up. "Really?"

"Yes," he laughs. "Really. The studio head was going to call, but I wanted it to be me. I hope you don't mind, but—"

"No, I—thank you." Emotion wells in my throat, and I whisper, "*You* did this for me. You made this happen."

"No, baby. You did this." His voice is warm, and there is pride etched in his tone. "All I did was get you the chance to be noticed. No one gets renewed for any reason but ratings. Tell your team, they just got job security. I'm going to come see you in a few when you break for lunch. I'll be out front. Congratulations, baby. I'm proud of you. See you soon." He disconnects, and joy fills me.

He's proud of me. I do not know why this matters to me so very much. But it does. It so does.

I draw in a breath and rotate to the room of watchful eyes. "We got an extra season renewal!"

The minute the words leave my mouth, the room breaks out in cheers. Dierk stands up and rounds the table, offering me his hand. He's a tall, good-looking guy with bleach-blond hair and striking blue eyes. "Congratulations."

I accept his hand. "Thank you." And when I pull back, he holds onto it and leans in close. "Let me take you out to dinner to celebrate."

My cheeks heat with this unexpected turn of events. "I'm very flattered, but I can't do that. I'm–well, I'm in a relationship."

He releases my hand, but he's studying me with intense scrutiny, as if he's going to say something else, which is probably because my decline was awkward. Not because I didn't want to decline, just the whole relationship statement is new to me. Good, but new. There's a shout of, "Everyone back in your places," which saves me from any further interaction.

Dierk and I quickly claim our seats, and it's not long before we're filming again, but there's an intensity in the way he's looking at me now. I'd be flattered, but I've found that since I hit the TV screen, powerful men are more interested in me. I'm not sure it's even a compliment when it's a status symbol for them. I'll stick with the man who knew me first when I had pigtails, not now that I'm in the spotlight.

The ease with which I reached this conclusion tells me a lot about how I really feel about me and Damion. All the struggles between us are about the outward influencers, not about us. I'd say that makes us solid, but nothing has really changed.

The same people who didn't want us together still don't want us together.

I guess it's not people. It's one person: Damion's father.

But he's as mighty a force as an army, and he and Damion are at war. That means I'm at war with him as well.

# Chapter Twenty-One

The rest of our morning footage is filmed rather quickly, and we break for lunch. The whole Dierk thing goes away rather easily when the cameras flip off and he is immediately pulled onto a business call. I hurry off toward my dressing room and text Damion on the way, eager to see him: *I'm done. Just changing clothes. I have a two-hour break.*

*I'm outside in a black SUV. I can't wait to see you, gorgeous.*

I smile, inside and out, at this new reality that is my relationship with this wonderful man: *I'll be there in ten.*

This afternoon is all rehearsals and voiceover work, which means I don't need to be fancy anymore. Once I'm in my dressing room, the scent of my gorgeous flowers teases my nostrils. With the reminder of Damion's sweetness, I flash back to the moment I'd heard Damion's voice on the other end of that call, in the middle of the studio. I'd been nervous, and yet, the thrill of his call had set butterflies dancing in my belly. I replay the conversation and thrill at the idea that he wanted to tell me about the renewal himself. His call, paired with an extra season renewal, is ridiculously validating. I'm wanted. I'm accepted. I'm good at what I do.

It's been a very long time since I felt those things.

And he's right. It's about ratings. This win is about me, and my team, killing the ratings, and for the first time since the show started, I allow myself to revel in that success. These things matter to me, and he clearly knew that. *You did this*, he'd said. *All I did was get you the chance to be noticed.* What felt like some sort of payment now feels like him showing faith in me.

With all of this in my mind, I'm over the moon.

I dress in my street clothes, grab my purse, and retrieve the ring and slide it back into place, a tightness in my chest knowing it's a ring Damion bought for me years ago. I allow myself only a moment to stare at it on my finger, before me and my grumbling belly hurry toward the exit. Once I'm outside, I'm greeted by a burst of golden sunshine splaying warmth over the city, and me. With a hand up to block the glare, I've just spied a driver standing next to an SUV when Dierk intercepts me, stepping directly into my path.

"Alana."

"Dierk," I say, aware of the way he towers over me in his ridiculously expensive suit, effectively blocking my view of the vehicle.

"I'm glad I caught you. I wanted to thank you for the invitation to the show. My mother is beside herself, and even more so, that she gets to come with me to look at properties with you next month. She feels like a movie star."

"I'm excited to meet her," I say, "and thrilled to give her the star treatment. I owe her for wrangling you into doing this."

"I'm glad she did as well." His eyes narrow. "That invitation to dinner—"

"Was appreciated, but as I said—"

"You're in a relationship," he supplies, and there is skepticism in his voice. "You told me that information in an awkward way. Why?"

It's a bold question, but my reply is fast and easy. "It's a new thing that was an old thing. But it's also a good thing." I motion behind him and choose my words cautiously so as not to invite scandal. "I actually have a driver waiting on me for a scheduled lunch."

He rotates just enough to bring the vehicle into his line of sight, and mine as well, and my breath hitches as I find Damion leaning on the SUV, his arms folded over his perfect chest, his chiseled jaw set hard in disapproval. Much like he did to my prom date, only Dierk is not the man in my life. Damion is, and he seems to be dead set on making that evident to Dierk.

Dierk's attention returns sharply to me. "You're seeing Damion West?"

I'm worried about Damion ending up all over the press because of me, and it somehow being used against him with his father. But with Damion standing there, staring at Dierk with a look that borders on downright violence, the message is clear. I am not to deny he's my man. And I really don't want to.

So I don't. Not really. But just as he was protecting me with the car service, I have to protect him, too. "I'm having lunch with him to celebrate our renewal," I reply.

"That's not an answer."

Dierk just won't let this go, and I think of how I would feel if I were Damion. I would not want to be denied. "Yes," I say. "I am. Nice to have you on the show, Dierk. See you next month." I end the conversation by stepping around him and walking toward Damion.

There's a predatory gleam in Damion's gaze, his anger crackling off of him, the wicked sweep of his gaze up and down my body, as possessive as it is bold. There is familiar jealousy in his behavior. Damion made a habit most of our youth of acting as if I were his girlfriend but then latching onto another woman—a complicated habit I can't say I didn't cause. I pushed him away. I called him "friend" and stressed how much I didn't want to lose our friendship. But this is not then, not even close, and his intensity is palpable.

I can feel Dierk at my back, watching us, and I don't know why I thought departing our conversation first was a good idea. He wants what Shauna wants—the scoop on my love life—and dread fills me. I'm going to pull Damion into the spotlight, and he's not that guy. What is he thinking, putting us on display as he is right here in this moment? He's watching my every step, staring at me like he wants to gobble me up or lick me all over, and there's no way anyone watching doesn't know—Dierk included.

I certainly know.

I'm melting like butter right here on this New York City street, my mind aiding in my body's seduction, replaying sexy moments, his hands and mouth on my body. Heat pools low in my belly, and my nipples pucker beneath my lacy bra. I'm an easy mark for the man who has been my fantasy all my life. I want him. I have always wanted him. Damion knows this, too, so I don't know why he feels this display is necessary, and while I might be warm all over, I don't like the head game it represents. Or that we are still in place after all these years to need to play them.

I halt a respectful distance in front of him, the wind teasing my nostrils with his familiar earthy scent and doing nothing to aid my efforts to chide him. "What are you doing?" I hiss, angry now, too.

He shackles my waist, and he tugs me into him, our legs intimately aligned.

"Making sure he knows you're mine," he answers boldly, a slight splay to his fingers.

It's all I can do not to touch him and add to the story any watchful eye is already writing about us. "You do realize we are all over the internet, and my producer wants to talk about us on air?"

"I don't care who knows, Alana. It's inevitable. We live together now. You're wearing my ring."

A not-so-nice feeling rips through my chest, right where my heart is. I forgot. The engagement show hasn't ended. He reads me instantly and cups my head. "Alana, baby, it's not fake."

My fingers curl into my palms, one on my purse and the other by my side. "Isn't it?"

"You're the most real thing in my life, Alana." His voice is low, roughened up. "Let's get inside the SUV." He pushes off the car and holds the door open for me, but I'm still living inside his words. I'm the most real thing in his life, and I'm still his fake fiancée, and I'm on display for the world to see. With this biting knowledge, I get in the SUV.

# Chapter Twenty-Two

My throat is raw with emotions as I settle against the soft leather of the seat, reminding myself that we are not fake. I am moving in with him. That's as real as it gets. I'm simply sensitive to this "fake" game we played after a lifetime of push and pull between us.

Damion joins me, shutting us inside. "We're ready," he calls out to the driver, his hand settling on my leg. "Have you ever been to Kristie's?"

That's it? Have I ever been to Kristie's? Really? I twist around and bring him into view, and I open my mouth to confront him, but then zip my lips. I'm aware of the driver, of the fact we are not alone, and anything I say to Damion could easily become fodder for the press as easily as it could standing beside the SUV outside.

He arches a brow.

I face forward again and fold my arms in front of me. "I heard it's fabulous. And close."

He captures my leg and drags me closer, his arm settling around me. "Don't be angry," he murmurs softly, his voice a seductive purr, "though my behavior is wholly your fault. You make me *that crazy*."

"I make you crazy?" I challenge, my voice low and filled with accusation. "As my mother would say: pot, kettle."

He laughs, and it's sexy and warm, as if we aren't even fighting right now. As if all of this amuses him. I reach over and press my hand to his leg, my fingers pressing deep. "That was not good what you did back there."

He covers my hand with his. "Just like old times, isn't it? Me misbehaving and you putting me in my place."

"That's not a good thing either."

Already, the driver is halting beside the restaurant, and Damion stuns me by catching me to him, cupping my head, and kissing me with a deep slide of his tongue that leaves me breathless and panting. "Everything about us is good, Alana," he murmurs, his thumb stroking lipstick from my bottom lip.

My fingers curl on his lapels. "We're going to talk about what just happened."

He catches my fingers with his. "I staked my claim, and I will do it over and over again until everyone knows you're mine. What else is there to talk about?" He doesn't give me time to argue, opening the door and exiting, taking me along with him.

A moment later, with my lips tingling from his kiss and my hand in his hand, he's helping me out of the backseat, and cameras are flashing. Lord, help us both, we're about to be tabloid fodder all over again. The press must have spied us back at the studio and followed. We're so close, they didn't even need to drive. They could have just ran after us on foot.

Damion pulls me in front of him, his big body a shield from the cameras. He's my shelter, and he's always been that to me, from everyone and everything but himself.

# Chapter Twenty-Three

A DOORMAN AND TWO security guards rush to our aid and usher us away from the flash of cameras and inside the shelter of the building. Relief washes over me with our escape, but in my mind, I'm already imagining the photos of me and Damion that will soon be blasted all over the internet. There's no way I'm avoiding the subject of "us" with the studio at this point. Zero. Zilch. Add another zero.

There's also no time to talk about this with Damion, as we're met by a tall, dark, and deadly-looking man in an expensive suit; he's accented with an earpiece. I'd label him as security, but his suit isn't just expensive—it's as expensive as Damion's. The man greets me with an incline of his chin. "Ms. Blue, I'm Adam. Nice to meet you."

"Hi," I say, confused and waiting for more information that doesn't follow.

Instead, he and Damion share a look, and there's a familiarity to their greeting that tells me these two are no strangers, and I'm being excluded from some invisible circle of knowledge. I eye the earpiece again, and Adam's towering height, his athletic build, and shark attention and concern fills me. He's a bodyguard, and there's a threat against Damion that requires Adam's presence, and it's downright unsettling.

Adam motions us down the hallway to the left and ultimately to a private elevator bank.

Once we're outside the one steel door and it's opened, Damion's hand settles on my lower back, urging me forward, and I step into the rather compact compartment. He follows, and when Adam joins us, his big body eating up considerable space, Damion responds by layering us up—stepping behind me, his hand pressed to my belly, my backside nestling his front. It's as if he's decided the entire world needs to know we're together, and, at present, I have a love/hate relationship with that concept.

Adam punches the button for the top level of the building, where the restaurant's legendary view and food will welcome us. The floors tick by rather slowly, and it's all I can do not to whirl on Damion and demand answers. What was that back there with Dierk? Who the heck is Adam, and why is he with us in this elevator?

Damion's fingers splay on my belly, almost as if he's warning me to wait, and the press of his flesh to mine is an unbidden distraction, conjuring images of us naked together only a few hours before. My nipples tingle and pucker, and my entire body trembles ever so slightly—so slightly no one would know, but *he* notices. I know Damion notices. I can feel the male satisfaction in him. He likes his power over me to stir this reaction at a time when we least want to have one.

But nothing he has done changes anything.

I'm still angry with him.

The elevator halts and opens, and Adam exits to allow ease of our departure. When I go to move, Damion's fingers once again flex where they hold me, a silent rejection of my escape, a reminder that we're being watched. I twist around and meet his stare, a burn in the depth of his I feel low in my belly.

"I'll explain," he promises, twining his fingers with mine before he lifts his chin toward the door.

The air between us crackles and snaps.

I want to hit him and kiss him and so many things, but all I do is nod, rotate, and exit the elevator with him on my heels and still holding onto me. We're greeted by a fifty-something woman with bouncy, red chin-length hair, her apron fitted snugly to a generous bosom. "Welcome, Mr. West and Ms. Blue." She motions to our left. "This way to your private dining space."

I glance at Damion, and I'm not surprised to find a dark, guarded look on his handsome face. It hits me then that he told me he wants to talk, and I'm starting to recognize a pattern in him. When there's something he's done that he knows displeases me or he dreads me knowing, he overcompensates for the negative. As he did by announcing our living arrangement to the guard as a show of his commitment. And perhaps today, with outward affection and a luxurious meal.

We're now following the redhead down the hallway, and I'm remembering the way he'd paid off my father's five-figure debt when we were only eighteen.

I'd been furious because of the timing. I'd just slept with him for the first time ever, after years apart from him, and I'd woken to a note, just a note. Damion had gone, leaving the country per his message, but he'd overheard a phone call between me and my mother. He'd figured out that my father owed money to gambling sharks. He'd gone on in the goodbye letter to inform me he'd paid off the debt. I'd been embarrassed, ashamed. Indebted to him. Even more so, I'd felt like he'd paid me for my services.

I felt like a hooker.

But with all I know now, it feels like so much more.

I'd thought he'd wanted to drive me away. And maybe that's true, but I think it might be a little more complicated than it seemed. There were a lot of ways he could have driven me away, and most of them didn't cost him five figures.

I glance behind me and find Adam standing at the elevator, on alert, spine stiff, and as tall as he is, in mile-high fashion. What is going on?

Rotating forward again, and just in time, the hostess halts us at an arched entry with glass doors and opens one. I'm finally only minutes from being alone with Damion.

# Chapter Twenty-Four

Tension curls low in my belly, and I enter our dining space.

It is, as promised, "private," with one single table in the center of the room and a wall of windows with enviable Central Park views even from a distance. The kind that costs millions in New York City. The kind that a meal with this view would be priced outrageously expensive and out of my budget, at least as long as I bleed money to my parents. But it's not out of Damion's budget, and not much is, I'm sure.

There are also only two seats, which seems to indicate Adam won't be joining us. Not that I'd expect security to join us, but I'm buzzing with a weird vibe over him that I can't seem to quite tamp down.

The table sits parallel to the windows, and Damion crosses the room and holds out a chair for me, inviting me to join him. The problem is that this placement will force my back to the door, and at present, Adam, I assume. I can't know for sure. I haven't looked behind me, and to do so would be ridiculously obvious. The control freak in me that's spinning out of control doesn't approve of this seating arrangement, but the only way to reject the seat is by indicating said rejection, and with an audience, that feels like yet more fodder for the gossips. I suddenly hate the idea that our entire lives are lived inside a looking glass. The billionaire and the TV personality on display. Anywhere we go, and all that we do, will always be on display.

Accepting the inevitable, I join Damion, casually glancing toward the door and noting Adam's absences, and doing so with unexplainable relief washing over me. I have no idea why he had me so very on edge, and all for naught, it seems. He *must* work for the building, and I've blown his presence into something bigger and darker. No longer bothered by the door at my back, I claim my seat, noting the champagne on ice I wish I could drink but don't dare when I still have to record speaking in coherent sentences this afternoon.

Damion rounds the table to sit across from me, the distance between us cozy, romantic even, which is confusing considering this is merely my lunch break and his, too. The woman in the apron, who I can now see sports a name tag that reads "April," reaches for the champagne. "May I pour?"

"I better not," I say, and glance in Damion's direction. "I have to work this afternoon and live with the words that come out of my mouth." I laugh. "If I drink, that won't be a fun thing to do. I'm sorry."

"Don't be sorry," Damion replies easily. "I should have known better. We'll come back for a full meal, including champagne. I *owe you*."

His voice is low, his tone as warm as the whiskey washing down my throat last night. His eyes are smoldering like a molten sunset, and I can't look away. He's not talking about dinner, but rather orgasms, and I can feel the heat rush to my cheeks.

"I can bring you whatever you like," April offers, and I jerk my attention in her direction, quickly filling the space between the exchange with Damion with basic meal talk.

"Unsweet tea now and coffee later with lots of cream and Splenda," I say. "I'll take Splenda for the tea, too, please."

"Of course." She replies with a nod and looks to Damion for his order. "For you, Mr. West?"

"Same. And Alana is crunched for time, so give us a few minutes, but she's going to want to order quickly."

"I'll be back with the drinks quickly, and then I can take your orders," April promises, and then she's walking toward the door.

The niceties and formality are over, at least for a few minutes, and I take advantage of what time we have alone, leaning into the table and closer to Damion. "What's going on? And what was that back there with Dierk?"

"I told you. I was staking my claim."

I swear my lips tingle with the memory of the kiss that followed that statement, but I stay focused on mining for information. He's not acting like himself. "I know what you said, but since when do you need to stake your claim on me, Damion? You left me alone for years. Now you're battling the green-eyed monster? It's illogical."

"You say that like I wasn't always battling the green-eyed monster with you, Alana. I wanted to beat the ass of every guy you dated."

I'd had this thought myself earlier, but as was the case in the past, I dismiss it now. "In a big brother way."

"I was never your brother. I never wanted to be your brother. I never willingly wanted to keep my hands off of you. But it was for the best. I'm a far better man now than I was then." His lips press together and thin. "I would have fucked up with you and lost you back then. I don't want to lose you, Alana." There's a grave quality to his voice. "Not ever."

My heart swells with his confession, but all these hints of a dark past claw at me. What was this past? What is it he doesn't want me to know about him? And do I care? It's not a question I need to think about for more than a few seconds: I don't. "You aren't going to lose me, Damion. I've been a sure thing since we were seven years old and kissing in the closet."

"You have never been a sure thing, Alana, not even when I kissed you before leaving for college."

"You were dating someone else," I argue. "You knew how I'd feel about that because you know me. You didn't want that to go anywhere."

He considers me for several long beats that feel as if they stretch eternally before he finally says, "You were always too good for me, Alana."

"I always felt like I wasn't good enough for you."

"The only reason that pleases me is that if you'd thought any different, you might have kicked me to the curb a long time ago. I'm still not good enough for you, Alana, but I have always been a better man when I'm with you. And we have always been damn good together." There is a rasp of emotion lacing his words that warns of so much more going on than what is on the surface.

And that very idea drives home my need to hold tight and hang on to him, and us. Protecting this bond between us feels more important than ever. "My producer is going to exploit us in every way possible. Are you really ready for how in our faces that will be?"

"Baby," he says, his voice softening and my belly trembling with the endearment he's using more and more these days. "I'm the heir to the West empire. I'm in the news far too often for my liking. It's nothing I'm not built for at this point."

"But you want to add more pressure on top of that?"

"It's a part of loving you, Alana. And it's a small price to pay. Keep us a mystery that drives your ratings but doesn't destroy our privacy."

"That's exactly what I'd thought, too, but my producer threatened to make me join a dating site if I don't give her more than hints about you. Or that's the general gist of it."

"Your producer is doing her job and acting like a ratings whore. Tell her no and mean it."

"She said my contract requires I give them pieces of my personal life. She wants to start with my parents. I don't think that's a good thing for me or us, Damion."

"If it gets your father too busy to gamble, it could be a good thing."

"What if they find out about the gambling?"

His lips press firmly together. "It'll only drive your ratings."

"Do you know how much I do not like that answer?"

"You didn't create this. He did. But stand your ground, Alana. Only give them what you want, how you want it represented. If you walk, the show ends, and so does her job."

"I hadn't thought of it that way. I'll be stronger, but it won't work if you act like you did today."

"He's a hound dog I know a little too well. He needed to know you're *mine*." I'm stunned by this proclamation, but even more so by the one that follows. "I do, too. And enough about that asshole, Dierk. I told you we need to talk, baby, and we do, now, before you go back to work."

That is, of course, when April decides to return with our drinks.

# Chapter Twenty-Five

I know Damion told me he wants to talk, but something about the way he announces it now, right before an interruption, is just plain killing me. My heart tangos right along with my emotions. This fancy lunch, Adam, and Damion's possessive behavior collaborate on a collective warning.

April sets the drinks in front of us and laces her fingers together over her apron. "Do we know what we want to eat?"

I sit back, forcing myself to breathe. Damion does not, his attention fixed on me as he says, "They have that strawberry salad you love, with pecan-crusted chicken. Everyone talks about it. That's why I brought you here." His voice is measured, his jaw tense, but there's a sense of urgency about him, as if he's eager to hurry her along.

"Perfect," I say agreeably, glancing at April. "I'll take that."

Still driving us forward, Damion adds, "The lemon chicken for me, sides as indicated on the menu. No salad." He hands her the menus, sending a clear message that we're done, and ready to be alone.

April proves she's skilled at reading a room and takes a rapid hint. "I'll get that going." She sets a small device on the table. "Buzz me if you need me." She flicks a look in Damion's direction. "Should I put the food in now or wait a few minutes?"

He glances at his watch and then back at her. "Wait ten minutes."

"Of course," she says, and pretty much darts for the exit.

I twist around to observe her departure, and the instant the door shuts with her on the other side, I rotate to Damion, urgency blasting through me like a shot of icy air. "Talk about what?"

"My father showed up at my attorney's office this morning. The same attorney that handled the contracts I made every board member voting with me sign."

On the surface, this is almost expected. It's his father, after all, but Damion's energy screams at me, warning there's more coming. "What else?"

He draws in a heavy breath and exhales before throwing his dart. "Your mother was with him."

It's a biting revelation, as my mother has promised me over and over she was done with Damion's father, but it's not as horrid as I'd expected. I know they're sleeping together. I know my parents are not happy together. My belief in fairy tale marriages and happy families ended years ago; sailed away on a ship filled with dreams and got lost one foggy Hudson Bay night years before.

And yet, I sit across from Damion, about to move in with him, with hope in my heart that we can be different. Perhaps I'm still a naïve little girl, but I'm not sure I want to become the alternative—a bitter, empty person.

"Alana?"

At Damion's prod, I blink him back into focus. "This isn't new. We know they're behaving badly. I just don't understand why she was with him there at your attorney's office."

His finely chiseled jaw flexes. "It was a message to me, Alana."

Unease sizzles through me. "What message?"

"He's close to you. He can get to you. And he'll use you to hurt me."

There's an ominous quality to his tone, but relief is fast and hard. I dismiss it with a wave of my hand. "But he can't, Damion. I told you. Nothing he can say—"

"You're wrong Alana, and we have to talk about how wrong, but not now, not in a public place. At home. *Our* home. And it has to be tonight. I'm only bringing this up now because we need to talk about protection."

My brows dip. "Protection? What does that even mean?"

"He'll try to drive you away from me, Alana, and if that doesn't work—"

"It *won't* work," I assure him.

"Desperate people do desperate things. If he fails to turn you against me, he'll do whatever it takes to break me, and the only way he does that is by hurting you. He knows that. That's why he stayed connected to your family."

I draw a hard-earned breath and try to digest what he's just told me. This is the pin in the happy balloon I'd been floating on when I'd walked into work this morning. "I'm your weakness. That's what you're telling me." My fingers curl on my lap. "Let me guess." My throat is tight, the words tight, my belly tighter. "You don't want me to move in with you. Is that what this is?"

He is on the floor on a knee beside me in an instant, tugging my chair around to face him, his expression as earnest as his words. "No. *No.* That is not what I am saying, woman. You're moving in with me, where you belong, if I have to hand pack your bags for you myself and throw you over my damn shoulder. You belong with me, Alana."

His reaction soothes the raw nerves the conversation has created, and I press my hand to his face. "I want so very much to be with you and to live with you, but you just told me I'm the blade that cuts you. I don't want to be that blade, Damion."

"He thinks you're a weakness, baby, but he's wrong. You're my reason to fight for right over wrong." He captures my hand and brings it to his lips. "You're moving in with me. Say it."

The words are a command, but there is trepidation in his eyes. He's fearful I will reject him, and it is not what he wants. This pleases me, it does. It is not what I want either, but I am worried beyond belief at all the ways he's placing himself in harm's way. "Answer honestly. Does me living with you make things harder on you? Does it make you more of a target?"

"You're already a target. You've always been a target. Strength in numbers."

"I didn't ask about me. I asked about you."

"I'm one of the few people safe from his wrath, at least for now. I'm the heir he wants to conform, not make go away."

"For now?"

"You're moving in with me. *Say it*," he repeats.

"Damion—"

"Nothing else divides, Alana."

"Right. You're right. Yes. I want to move in with you. I've been excited about it all morning long."

"Good. One more thing, though."

"Do I want to know?"

"Probably not, so I'll just tear off the band-aid. The minute he knows you stand by me and can't be swayed to step away, he'll act quickly and swiftly. I need to know you're protected. You need a bodyguard."

"What? No. Wait." I blink and will my thundering heart to calm. "I'm just putting this all together. You think...he'll try to kill me?"

# Chapter Twenty-Six

*Y*OU THINK...HE'LL TRY TO *kill me?*

"Not yet," Damion replies.

"Not yet?" I gasp and pop to my feet, Damion following me. "Not yet?" I repeat. "Are you *serious?*"

His hands settle on my shoulders. "Easy, sweetheart. It's always best to plan for the worst. That's where my head is."

"Has he killed other people?"

"I'm protecting you. That's all you need to know right now."

My hand balls between my breasts. "That's a yes. Who? How? How do you know?" I grab his lapels. "*Why?*"

"He's vicious, Alana. That's all I can tell you right now. The rest has to be when we're alone, at home, our home."

*Our home.*

The way he says those words, in a roughened-up voice leaden with emotion, almost scares me more than anything else he's said to me. He's worried. Really worried, and I think of his statement about losing me. He needs me with him, but more so, he fears his father will win, and I'll leave him. I wrap my arms around him and hold him tight, pressing my head to his chest, and before my chin lifts, my gaze finds his.

"At home," I whisper. "I just hate that you have hours to worry over what I'll think about whatever you have to tell me."

"I just told you my father might try and kill you, and you're worried about me." His forehead presses to mine. "I do not deserve you."

I press my hands to his face. "Stop saying things like that already. We'll get through this." I pull back to look at him. "We're finally together."

"And I want to keep it that way," he says. "I hired Adam to be your bodyguard. He's a retired Navy SEAL and works for an operation I trust. He's your shadow until further notice. He's elite. He will keep you safe."

"Why do I need someone of that caliber?"

"Because the man who works for my father is of that caliber."

My mouth goes dry, cotton thickening my words. "And he'd—*kill* me?"

"I believe he'd kill for money. Adam is necessary. When we're done eating, I'll bring him in and we can talk to him together."

Obviously, there was a reason Adam set me on edge, and it had nothing to do with him and everything to do with Damion's father. Even so, there's still a part of me that wants to reject this idea of such an invasion of privacy, but I'm not a fool any more than Damion is an exaggerator. I give a tiny nod of my head. "Yes."

He strokes hair behind my ear, the tender touch sending a shiver down my spine. "It's going to be okay," he promises.

I catch his hand and pull it between us. "You need to remember that, too. But will he ever stop coming for us?"

"He will." His voice is pure steel, but he offers nothing more, and I'm just not in the mindset to accept that answer.

"How?" I ask, pressing him.

"I have a plan. *Trust me.*"

"We do this together. I want to know the plan."

"Tonight. We have a lot to talk about, but it has to be *tonight*."

There's a heaviness to that repeated statement, a darkness that twists me in knots. Just what is it he has to tell me that he can't share here?

"Right now, let's enjoy lunch together," he adds, pulling my chair out for me again.

I'm not sure that's even possible, but his eyes, his energy, compel me to sit down. I do as he's bid, settling into my seat, and he scoots me to the table again, and I have this sense of him using that act to rein in control.

I shiver and hug myself. He's scared. And because he's scared, I am, too.

# Chapter Twenty-Seven

Our food arrives immediately after we sit, and it's as if we've made a concerted effort to disappear into the moment together. We dig in, and after a few bites, we're already chatting up a storm. We decide fairly promptly that we must return one evening when we're not rushed. "And when I can try their famous mac n cheese and take a nap after," I say. "Joking. Okay, I'm serious. I will eat all the pasta and need to be rolled home."

"You and your mac n cheese. You are forever obsessed. I can make us reservations for Saturday night if you want."

"I'd love that," I say. "I'd ask to try your chicken, but you ate it all."

"Shit. I did. I should have offered."

I laugh. "I'm teasing you. You know I don't love chicken."

He laughs now, too, and the thing is, despite all that is happening in our lives, it feels good to remember how good we are together and how well we know each other, too. We're that good together. Because we've known each other a lifetime, and I've never been more comfortable with a man in my life and yet so darn attracted to him, too.

"I remember exactly what ruined chicken for you." Amusement lights his eyes.

"Oh yeah," I say, "prove it."

"Because we went to that buffet years ago, and your chicken squirted blood."

I cringe just hearing it. "Yes. It was so horrible." I scrunch my face up. "It was really, really gross."

"You were traumatized."

"Still am."

He laughs and shakes his head. "I should have given you some of my chicken. You'd forget the buffet. It was that good. Next time." He sips his drink and asks, "How was your morning?" And the thing about the question that makes it matter is that I believe he really wants to know. It's in his eyes, in the way he watches me and waits for my answer.

When I'm with him, and this dates back to childhood, I feel like he narrows his massive world and makes it all about me. It's not something I've ever felt with anyone but him.

"Good," I say. "I filmed the intro for several episodes."

"Are you done with Dierk now?"

I laugh and shake my head. "Are you really jealous?"

"As fuck." He shoves aside his empty plate and laces his fingers together on the table. "He's a hound dog. Are you done with him?"

"No. We film the second half of his episode in about a month, but his mother will be chaperoning."

"I'm not sure that matters."

"Is he that much of a hound dog?"

"Most men are until they find the right woman." His eyes dance with mischief as he adds, "Or until they finally convince her to move in with them."

My stomach flip-flops at the reference to me being the right woman. "You *were* a hound dog. Big time. You kissed me while with another woman."

"Girl," he amends. "She was a girl. We were teenagers, and for all I knew, I'd never see you again. I was standing there, trying to say goodbye without touching you, but I couldn't." His voice lowers, a smoky quality to it, as he adds, "It felt like walking away without kissing you would have been one of the biggest mistakes of my life."

Emotion thickens my throat at the idea that he cared that much about me, and I never believed it to be true. I let insecurity frame too much of my life. "It all worked out."

"Not quite yet, baby, but I'm working really damn hard to fix that. Can I bring Adam in now?"

At that whiplash change of subject, nerves erupt in my belly at the idea of some strange man following me around. "Do we have to?"

"Yes. We have to." He glances at his watch. "It's late, and I want to lay the groundwork between you two while I'm present."

I shove my plate aside now as well. "He needs a chair, I guess."

"I'll get him and a chair," he says, "and I already told him you're hands off."

My eyes go wide. "No, you didn't. Please tell me you didn't say that to that man!"

He laughs a low, raspy, sexy laugh I feel low in my belly. "You're a beautiful woman, Alana. You're damn straight, I did." He pushes to his feet and walks to the door, leaving me as mortified as I am blown away by his possessiveness.

I'm not sure if that says he's all in, or if this threat from his father has him unnerved and acting out of character, or both.

Either way, the door opens, and I push to my feet to find Adam entering the room with Damion on his heels, no chair in sight. Which is probably for the best, as I have to go back to work.

I turn to greet both men. Adam inclines his chin in my direction. "Ma'am."

"Hi," I say, lifting my hand and then hugging myself. "I really hate this."

"Understandable, considering trouble is the reason you're stuck with me, but the good news is I'm really good at kicking trouble's ass."

Damion steps to my side and slides his arm around me, tilting his head low to speak to me and me alone. "I met with him before lunch and filled him in on everything. And everything means *everything*. Your father. My father. Your mother."

"Oh," I say, the soap opera that is our life is so damn embarrassing I want to crawl under the table.

My gaze lifts to Adam's again, which means I tilt my chin all the way up. The man is incredibly tall, even more so than I'd thought before lunch, which lends itself to a concern. I twist around to face Damion. "He's a very big man. And noticeable. He's going to get attention. He's going to be all over the press, right along with me."

"High-profile people have bodyguards all the time," Damion argues. "He'll stay in the background every occasion he can."

"What am I supposed to tell my producer?" I counter.

"It's already handled," he informs me. "I made that call and told them you have a stalker."

I bristle at this information. "Do you think you should have talked to me first?"

"Baby, I'm trying to protect you."

"I get that, but talk to me first," I chide.

"If this wasn't necessary—"

"Damion, *talk to me first*."

His expression tightens. "Understood. In my defense, I just want you safe."

I soften with this admission and catch the lapels of his jacket. "I know. I do, but there are assumptions about me and my career that come with my relationship with you."

"We talked about this—"

"I know. I do. I just know how gossip will fly."

"I promise to be discreet," Adam interjects. "And keep you safe. Do you know how to shoot a gun?"

I rotate to face Adam again. "I don't, and I really don't want to, either. The idea of holding a weapon that could kill someone scares me."

"We should teach you to shoot and get you a handgun," Adam says as if I said nothing at all, his attention shifting to Damion. "I can take her to the shooting range and teach her."

"I'll teach her," Damion replies. "We'll go tomorrow."

I cut Damion a stare. "You shoot?"

"Yes." That's all he says, but his jaw flexes, and he cuts his gaze as if there's something in his eyes he doesn't want me to read.

Unbidden, a chill races down my spine. He's warned me that there are bad things in his past, and for the first time, I wonder just how close to hell Damion got before he came back to Earth.

Damion's hand settles on my lower back. "Grab your stuff, and let's hit the road."

There's this edge to him now, near coldness, I see for what it is. His wall he uses to protect himself and me. The problem is, I think he's protecting me from himself, and I don't know how that works out well for either of us.

It's trouble.

The kind Adam can't save us from.

# Chapter Twenty-Eight

We exit the building to a chilly afternoon that contrasts the heated frenzy of the press, way beyond anything I've ever experienced. Once Damion, Adam, and I have escaped the craziness and are safely tucked inside the vehicle, with Adam in a seat facing us, I pant out a breath. "What is happening?" I say, exasperated by just how deep the reporters had stood. "I've never had this kind of press. Ever." I twist around to face Damion. "It's because we were caught on camera last night, isn't it?"

"I'm fairly certain that's accurate," he says tightly. "It'll wear off after a bit."

"You see what I mean? Our relationship is going to haunt you, Damion."

Shadows dance across his features, and he reaches up and strokes my cheek. "You've been haunting me my whole life, and I like it."

"Damion," I breathe out, overwhelmed with emotion at his response and awkward at Adam's presence. It's weird being watched and having someone in our intimate space.

"Baby, I promise you I'm up for this, if you're up for the ride I'm about to take you on, too."

I forget Adam and slide my hand into his. "I am, and I wish you knew that."

"You'll show me. We got this. I promise."

I swallow the new wave of emotion he's stirred. *We got this. I hope so*, is all I can think. *I really, really hope so.* Those words, and this man, slide inside me, settle deep in my soul, and fill me up where I have been empty and alone for a very long time. All my life, I've been battling an uphill battle and doing it alone. But I'm not alone anymore. And maybe I never was. He was out of sight, but never out of mind or reach.

"We do," I promise, and already the vehicle is approaching the studio.

Adam turns to the driver, saying something to him before he addresses me. "We're going to get out at a coffee shop down the road. I know the owners. We'll slip out the back door before they know we're gone. You'll need to leave us there, Damion."

"I'd rather drop her at the door," Damion argues.

"I know," he says, "but this is the best way to throw them off your trail for the rest of the day."

I squeeze Damion's hand. "I'm fine. I have Adam to keep me safe, because you made sure I have Adam."

The SUV halts in front of the coffee shop. I lean over and press what is meant to be a quick kiss on Damion's mouth. He catches the back of my head and licks into my mouth, a short, drugging kiss before he says, "Text me when you're in the building."

"I will," I promise.

"I'll pick you up, and we'll go get your things on the way home."

"Yes," I whisper, and rotate away from him, facing Adam. "I'm ready."

He nods and opens the door, exiting before me and then waving for me to join him. Once we're on the sidewalk, he shuts Damion inside the vehicle, and he guides me forward and into the coffee shop. It's a dauntingly short jaunt, and for the first time in my life, I'm nervous out in public, like I should be expecting bullets to fly. The press doesn't bother me; that man working for Damion's father does.

I need Adam close because of him.

I need Adam, because I'm in real danger.

The doors of the coffee shop close behind us, and the scent of coffee beans and cinnamon tease my nostrils. Glancing about, I find a cozy, welcoming little joint with shelves filled with adorable mugs and trinkets, and relief washes over me. We're sheltered now. We're fine.

Adam waves at a gorgeous brunette behind the counter and points at the door. "Cover us," he calls out.

"Anything for you, blue eyes," the woman replies, rounding the counter and heading for the door.

Adam motions me forward. "Keep moving."

So much for sheltered.

In a blink, we're outside again, walking down an alleyway I didn't know existed, but it somehow feels safer than the main street. I glance around, looking for a threat.

"We're fine," Adam promises.

"I know," I say, because I'm trying to convince myself it's true, and then, needing a distraction, I ask, "She's pretty. Is she your girlfriend?"

He laughs, and it's a friendly laugh. "No. One of my friend's wives."

"Oh," I say. "That's cool that she obviously likes you."

"You never want your friend's wife to hate you or like you too much. Those are good ways to end up with no friends."

My mind goes to Andrew, a friend of Damion's who I went out with one time after he left for college. Even after Damion kissed me that day while still dating another girl, I'd felt so very guilty. The same was not true of Andrew, but I cut things off, nice and clean. They're still friends today, which I know because Andrew later called me and thanked me for keeping him from making a stupid mistake.

"Does your friend work with you?" I ask, refocusing on Adam.

"Yes. Walker Security is a lifestyle, not a job. We all live, work, and play together. We try not to die together." He halts us at the studio and runs a key card across a security panel that opens the door. Obviously noting the surprise in my eyes, he explains, "I'm cleared to go wherever you go. Now get in there and do your job. I'll be on set and nearby if you need me."

I huff out a breath. "I'm not looking forward to explaining you to the crew."

"Then don't. One thing I've learned is that sometimes less is more."

*Just not with Damion*, I think, nodding and walking inside the building. I can feel him at my back as we climb a narrow set of steps, and it's just weird having a shadow. Fortunately, we arrive at the top level, right next to the hallway to my dressing room. I turn to Adam. "I need to put my things in my dressing room. Then I go to the sound studio."

"I'll wait outside your door."

"This is just...strange. You know it's strange, right?"

"Safe is not strange, but I hear dead is." He motions to the ring on my finger. "How are you going to marry your man if you're dead?"

He's hit a nerve ten feet wide. I'm not supposed to marry him at all. "Right," I say. "I'd like to not be dead just yet." With a queasy feeling in my belly, I rotate on my heels and all but fly down the hallway, and even so, Adam is there before me.

"I need to check the room first."

*Oh my God*, I think, but I give a choppy nod. He opens the door and enters, and only moments later, he announces, "Clear," steps aside, and motions me into the dressing area.

"Thank you," I say, and walk inside, but just as I shut the door, a thought hits me, and I rotate to Adam again. "Is Damion in danger?"

"He hasn't given me reason to believe he needs protection."

"I don't agree with that assessment. He's too macho to think he needs it. He can protect himself, is how he will think. I don't even have to ask. Talk him into it, please. His father is a monster."

He offers me a half-lidded, impossible-to-read stare, a beat passing before he says, "I'll see what I can do."

I nod again and enter the room, shutting the door behind me and just leaning on it for a moment that turns into a few. I can't believe where we've landed and what all of this has become. My gaze catches on the flowers. I never even thanked Damion. I reach into my pocket and pull out the card and read the typed note, ice rippling down my spine: *What I give, I can take away.* There's no signature, but I know who sent the flowers. It was Damion's father.

# Chapter Twenty-Nine

I start pacing, my mind a jumbled mess as I struggle to process the implications of the flowers and the note, my heart beating uncomfortably fast through my mental freakout. What is this? What is going on? I halt and read the typed message again: *What I give, I can take away.*

What the heck does that even mean?

My hand swipes at a wayward lock of brown hair and I shove it behind my ear. I press my fingers to my forehead and then drop them. Is he talking about Damion? Or maybe the money he gave my father? My show? My show would be the least of my worries if it weren't for the fact that there are many jobs attached to its production. Losing it doesn't just impact me. It impacts them. It would impact so many people, including my parents, which would be a way he could take away in so many ways.

I fall back into my chair in front of my dressing table and think about what I learned at lunch. Damion's father took my mother to the attorney's office today, knowing Damion would find out. The timing cannot be a coincidence. That warning Damion spoke of wasn't just for Damion about me. It was for me. He must be threatening my parents. I throw the piece of paper, and as if taunting me, all it does is catch in the air and fall toward the ground right in front of me. I can't make it, or the content of the note, go away.

Launching myself to my feet again, I have no idea what to do with my nervous energy or how to handle this. I know Damion, and if I tell him about his father's threat, he's going to be beyond furious, and I cannot sit in a soundproof booth without going crazy. My mind goes to Adam, just outside my dressing room door, and I consider telling him what I've discovered, but he works for Damion; he'll tell him. I know he'll tell him. I glance at my watch, and my stress ratchets up ten levels. I have five minutes until my call time. I have to make a decision.

No matter how bad this gets, I can't *not* tell Damion. He'd never forgive me for holding this back, and that's a trust issue I don't think we need between us.

I grab my phone from the dressing table and punch in his number. The call lands directly to voicemail, and I'm ridiculously relieved yet fretful. I have no time, and I hurry to the door and open it. Adam is immediately standing in front of me. "Ready?"

"No. Come inside. It's urgent. And we need privacy."

His expression is stone. "I don't think that's a good idea."

"Oh my God, Damion and his threats." I throw my hands up in the air. "I know you aren't after my body, Adam. I have minutes to get to my call time. Come in now." I back up, and, thankfully, he steps inside.

"Shut the door," I order, bending down to pick up the note, and when we're sealed inside alone, I hand it to him. "Look at this."

His brows dip, but he accepts the piece of paper and reads, his gaze shooting to mine. "What is this?"

"This morning, I received flowers. I thought they were from Damion. I was late and didn't look at the card until now." I motion to the note he holds. "That's not from Damion."

His gaze darts to mine and narrows. "Who is this from?"

"His father," I say, hugging myself. "I know it's from his father."

He shoots a photo of the note and hands it back to me. I wave it off, wanting nothing to do with the threat I cannot truly escape, but at least I don't have to fretfully read it over and over if it's with him, not me. "What did he give you that he's threatening to take away?" he asks.

I tunnel my fingers through my hair in utter frustration. "I've been trying to figure that out. Damion? My show? He doesn't have the direct power to cancel us, but he bribes everyone. He can get to anyone, it seems. Or maybe it's the money my father borrowed? Or even my mother? I don't know; I really don't, but none of these possibilities are good for me and those around me. They hurt someone other than myself—all of them—which means I can't just blow this off. And I think it's important to note that I found the flowers in my dressing room right about the time he paraded my mother in front of Damion's lawyer."

"Does Damion know?"

"I can't reach him, and I have to report to my call time." I glance at my watch. "Now. I have to go now."

I try to step around him, and he catches my arm. "I have to tell Damion."

"Tell him. He's going to lose his shit though, so make sure someone is with him to pull him off his father."

His lips press together. "I'll handle it once we get you to the studio."

"How? You're stuck here with me."

"I'll handle it."

"I'll be in a soundproof booth. No one can get to me there. I'll be in there for hours. I'll be safe, locked down even. You can go handle this, and I'll be fine."

"We have a second man on his way over. I'm not leaving you alone."

"A second man is a little excessive, don't you think?" I challenge.

"No," he says, offering nothing more, and I can't help but wonder what he knows that I do not.

He opens the dressing room door, surveys the hallway, and then motions me forward. I glance at my ring, and consider removing it, but decide against it. It makes me feel close to Damion and I need that right now. I step out of the room, and join Adam. Side by side, we travel toward my destination, and when we're finally there, thankfully everyone else is already inside, and I hold up a hand to Adam. "You can't go inside. This is the actual recording studio."

"I'll need to clear your location. That's non-optional. The studio is aware of my presence. They've approved me to do what I need to do."

"Adam—"

"Alana," he counters. "I'm going to clear the room, or you're not going in." There's an absoluteness to his tone. Damion hasn't just paid him to protect me. Instinctively, I know he's threatened him, though I have a sense that neither of those things matter to Adam. What does is how much I mean to Damion to make him do those things.

I draw in a breath and nod. He opens the door to my destination, steps inside, and, after about sixty seconds, returns. "Clear."

"Thank you," I say softly. "I know you're just trying to help. I don't mean to be difficult. I'm just not used to—well, all of this."

"And we're going to do our best to ensure you don't need to get used to any of this. We'll help Damion make it go away. He loves you."

His words matter to me, especially the part where it's obviously enough that he knows Damion loves me, but I've never really questioned that love. We've always loved each other. There have just always been obstacles between us, and every moment I'm reminded that nothing has changed.

"I love him, too," I whisper. "Very much." I rotate away from Adam and step to the door, pausing to calm my nerves and steel myself for what comes next.

Dread fills me at the million questions I will face inside, but a part of me is now quite relieved that Adam is present. He's an extension of Damion, who is finally back in my life after years of back and forth and turbulent times. But I cannot help but feel I'm the catalyst for something dark and dangerous, and perhaps destructive.

Maybe I should have stayed away from Damion, and him me, but I'm objective enough to know that was never going to happen. We were always going to find each other again, and this time it means war. My fear, which evidently echoes that of Damion's and now Adam's, is that our love is going to turn bloody.

# Chapter Thirty

The minute I'm inside the soundproof booth, Lana corners me. "You have a stalker?"

"Seems that way," I eek out, steeling myself for the questions to follow.

"And you didn't tell me that?"

"I was trying to downplay it, but it seems that just won't be possible."

"What happened?"

My mind races for a story to control her and keep her far from the truth. "The kicker was the flowers I got today with a rather scary coded message. Damion decided it was time to act, and he approved it with the studio."

"Do you know who it is?"

"No," I say, because, truly, I'm only guessing that it's his father. Even though I guessed right, of course.

Her eyes light. "What if we—"

"No. No is the answer to what you're about to ask. What happens when you trigger this person and they attack me, or even you? And what would the insurance company for the production say?"

"You're going to have to give me something juicy sooner rather than later. You know that, right?" She doesn't wait for an answer. "Let's get to work."

Three hours later, we still have at least an hour to record, when I finally get a break that allows me to step out of the sound booth. I dart out of the room to find Lana talking to Adam. "Why not?" Lana asks.

"Why not what?" I ask, trying to figure out how she got here so much faster than I did.

"She's trying to talk me into being on your show," Adam supplies.

"I told you no, Lana," I say, and I am not pleased. "No does mean no."

"He's hot," Lana says. "There'd be ridiculous gossip about you two, and it would take pressure off Damion."

I'm not one to pull rank, even Damion's rank, but I'm at my limit. "Lana, I think you're forgetting who Damion is. He's worried enough about this to want to pause production."

This has her eyes flying wide. "What? No. That would cost a fortune."

"Ask a man with his kind of money if he cares. I assure you, he'll say no when it comes to my safety."

She flips this around on me. "How hot and heavy are you two?"

"I'm moving in with him."

She shakes her hand. "Hot, hot, and hot. Does the studio know?"

"He is the studio." I cast Adam a pleading look. "Can we talk alone?"

"Of course."

I start walking, and he follows until we're several feet from Lana, who crosses her arms in front of her and just watches us. I offer her my back. "She's making me crazy."

"I can see why, but you handled it well."

"You think?" I ask, needing that reassurance when I'm in uncharted waters. "Damion will approve. I hope so. We've had very little time to talk about all of this. Did you show him the card from the flowers?"

"I did. He says his father is contained."

"Contained? What does that even mean?"

"I think it's best if he explains, but he said to tell you to relax. He's got this handled. All is well. He sent you a message."

I snake my purse from my shoulder, where I stuffed my phone after silencing it, and yes, there's a message from Damion: *Remember when you used to make me prove you could trust me by falling back into my arms? You can trust me. I promise you, I have this handled. I will not let my father get in between us again. Ever. I'm in meetings all afternoon, one that will run until about seven. Walker will get you to your former apartment. Pack up. I'll pick you up there, and then we can go HOME and order pizza and get naked. I'm crazy about you. See you soon.*

I stare down at the message and sink into a memory from the past. I have fallen backward and know Damion will catch me. And he had. But when he wanted to do the same with me, I was afraid he was too big and I was too small for me to actually catch him. I'm still afraid of the exact same thing. There is a dark side to Damion—a dark past I don't begin to understand—that I feel in my gut could come back to haunt him. What if he's so busy trying to protect me that he falls, and I don't know how to catch him?

# Chapter Thirty-One

It's after five, and I'm in my dressing room gathering my things, and those damn sweet flowers bite at my senses and just drive me crazy. I shove my purse onto my shoulder, open one of the dressing room tables, pull out a candy bar, and exit the dressing room to where Adam waits on me. I offer him a Mr. Goodbar, my personal favorite. "Can I bribe you to throw these damn flowers away?"

"As much as I want that candy bar—I'm starving—I can't leave you to throw them away."

I blow hair from my eyes. "Take it anyway. You deserve it for putting up with me and Lana."

He accepts the bar and rips it open. "Thanks," he says, already shoving a big chunk in his mouth. "Can you leave a note for janitorial?"

"I should just give them to someone." Right about then, Lana heads our direction.

I groan. "Not again. I need a bite of that candy bar."

He holds it out, and I break off a bite and shove it in my mouth. "Don't look like you just saw your worst nightmare," Lana reprimands. "I know I'm a ratings whore, but I'm just trying to keep us all working. I came to apologize. I know having a stalker is scary. I'll do better. You want me to get rid of those flowers?"

"Yes. Please. I hate the smell. I never want to see another rose in my entire life."

Lana surprises me and pulls me into a hug. "I'm a bitch. I'm sorry." She catches my shoulder and pulls back to look at me. "And we got an extra season, babe. You're rocking it."

"We're rocking it," I say. "And I appreciate your hard work. We wouldn't be here without your skill."

"Thanks for saying that, Alana. We're a good team. Go get some rest." She winks. "Tell Damion I said hi."

I shake my head at her and say, "You just can't help yourself, can you?"

"I wouldn't be me if I could. Go home."

I motion to Adam, and we fall into step together. "We have a ride waiting," he informs me. "Damion said you need to go to your old place and pack up."

I laugh. "Did he really call it my old place?"

"Isn't it?" he asks.

"As of this morning, when I said yes to moving in."

"Sounds like a man who doesn't plan on letting you forget you said yes."

He's not wrong, and this warms me in all kinds of ways. I settle into the backseat of an SUV with Adam in the front next to a driver, a man with dark, wavy hair and a muscular frame, who lifts a hand and eyes me over his shoulder. "I'm Kelvin, also with Walker. Nice to meet you."

"Nice to meet you," I say, but I'm uneasy over just how much manpower is going into protecting me. Damion says he's got everything under control. He tells me not to worry, but he's clearly worried, and in a big way.

The vehicle begins to move, and my cellphone rings. Hoping it's Damion, I retrieve my phone from my purse to feel a punch in the gut at the sight of my mother's number. After what Damion told me at lunch, I'm in knots just thinking about talking to her, afraid to hear what she will say. But I'm also afraid of what I need to know and might not if I don't answer.

I swallow the cottony sensation in my mouth and answer. "Hello, Mother."

Kelvin and Adam don't react, but I can almost feel their unease, their alertness. They believe my mother is a threat, and I don't know what to do with that information.

"Hi, honey." Her voice trembles, and I steel myself for what's coming. "Your father and I had a major fight. I really need to talk. I need to get him under control once and for all before something really bad happens to him."

My world spins with her words, and with the implications behind them that are so much worse after I found out she was with Damion's father this morning. Anger burns in my belly and roars to life, but I manage a cool voice as I ask, "What does that even mean? *Before something really bad happens to him?*"

# Chapter Thirty-Two

At this point, Adam is leaning around the seat, questions burning in his gaze, but I'm focused on my mother. "What's going to happen to Dad, Mom?" I press.

"I just—he's gambling too much. We're both enabling him, and I don't know how to make it stop. Can you just come over? I'm shaken by how intensely we fought."

Bitterness overwhelms me. I've given up everything in reply to her tears and her begging. The truth is, it's rarely my father who asks for my help. It's her, and after what I found out today, I'm feeling pretty darn done.

"I'm not coming over," I say, surprising myself, so I am certain she is stunned. "I'm moving in with Damion. I have to get packed and moved."

"You're what? What are you talking about?" Her tone is biting, angry, and I cannot help but wonder if the source is Damion's father's influence or her fear of Damion's influence on me.

"Oh, please, Mother. You're well aware of the fact that I've been in love with him my entire life. I told you I was going to marry him when I was seven."

"That was a kid thing! I never thought you'd really marry that man. He was always destined to be just like his father."

Anger and adrenaline rip through me, and it's all I can do to hold back an accusation. I thank the reserve the camera has taught me, as I know anything I say to her will be used against Damion.

I burn to say something snippy, for instance, "If you weren't in bed with his father, maybe you'd be paying attention to what's going on in your daughter's life a little more closely," but I do not. "Whatever the case," I say instead, the pinch in my chest threatening to create a burn in my eyes, "I'm moving in with him."

"He's a player, a manwhore." Her tone is incredulous. "He's going to fuck you over and laugh about it. The little girl next door who pants after him. Do you want to be that?"

Her words bite and grind and I feel myself go cold inside, but not because I believe her words. Because she actually said them. "Be careful what you say about Damion to me, Mom. I love him, and you need to be clear: I will fight for him. You need to understand that means *at all costs*."

Seconds tick by before she issues a tightly spoken, "I see," and I can only assume she's wondering how weird this gets since she's in the wrong bed and on the wrong side of everything.

I don't think she sees anything but her own personal agenda. "What was the fight with Dad about?"

"You know what the fight was about. I need help managing him."

"He's a grown adult."

"With an addiction, and I don't know what to do anymore."

That's it. I hit a wall. "Try making different decisions, and I'm fairly certain you know exactly what I'm talking about, because this is about to get embarrassing. My producer now wants to delve into my parents' personal lives. She believes there to be a juicy scandal there. Think about that tonight. Think hard about where that leads when the press starts following you." I hang up.

The vehicle halts in front of my building, my cell hums again, and caller ID alerts me to yet another call from my mother. I hit decline, and the passenger door opens. Kelvin appears in my line of sight, concern etched in his dark eyes, and geez, are all the Walker men big bad asses with good looks? Because, as is the case with Adam, Kelvin is all of those things.

"Sucks really badly when parents suck," he says. "Sorry that you're dealing with this, but please know we're here to help."

I wonder if he speaks from personal experience, but I don't know him well enough to ask. Whatever the case, there's a genuineness about Kelvin and Adam that is appreciated so very much right now, but it also drives home how little of that quality has been in my life. Damion has changed that for me in all kinds of ways.

Adam appears opposite Kelvin's position, both men framing me, a shelter that I am certain is intentional. Damion has told them what he told me. His father would cause me harm to cause him harm. I'm angry with my mother—furious in fact—but I'm officially concerned about the easy target she's made of herself. "I need to know what just happened," Adam states.

I'm oddly without resistance to his nosing into my personal matters. "She said they were fighting, I suspect about her seeing Damion's father again, but she claims it's about my father's gambling. It might be. He has a real problem."

"Gambling leads to debt with the wrong people," Kelvin comments grimly. "Sounded like she was mentioning some type of danger?"

"Yes," I agree wholeheartedly. "But take that concern with a grain of salt. They've used the threat of owing money to the wrong people against me my entire adult life. Damion even bailed them out years ago. I'm not sure I'm objective enough to know if any of it is real anymore."

"We can find out," Adam assures me, "but you need to know, we don't have anyone watching them at present. We didn't commit to taking them on until next week. Under the circumstances, I'll see if we can step that up."

"Our team should, at the very least, be able to get eyes on them by way of street and building cameras, as well as online activity," Kelvin adds.

"Agreed," Adam replies. "We'll get a look at what went down at your parent's building today."

"I'm not as worried about the gambling as I am Damion's father." I hug myself, embarrassed about my mother's behavior. "She's sleeping with him. She can't even see how she's being used. If Damion's father can't get to me, why wouldn't he just hurt her? My devastation would be Damion's torture."

Adam and Kelvin exchange an unreadable look before Adam says, "We'll get someone on her quickly." He motions to the building. "I'm going up with you."

It's all they're going to say, but I feel like it's enough. They get it. I know they get it. I nod in Adam's direction without argument. At this point, I've accepted Adam and the need for security. I'm also comforted by knowing Adam is a highly skilled professional. We enter my building into a simple lobby without security, and Adam glances over at me. "You know you need a layer between you and any potential threat, right?"

I stab at the elevator button. "It's never been a problem until now, and I'm moving in with Damion anyway."

The doors open, and we step inside the car, where I press in my floor. "You've been lucky," he says, obviously not ready to let this go. "I've seen people with much less fandom than you have some pretty scary things happen. Not everything is about luxury. Some things, like your choice of residence, become about safety."

"I appreciate your concern, but it's moot. I really am moving in with Damion now, tonight."

"Damion doesn't make your decisions for you. The best influence I can have on you is to ensure you make the right ones."

I rotate to face him. "Okay, then, let's talk about decisions. Do you think I should have gone to see my mother tonight?"

If he's shocked by the change of subject or the personal nature of my question, he doesn't so much as blink. "From a safety perspective, no. Based on my limited knowledge of your circumstances with her, I still say no, and that's not personal. I don't like volatile unknowns inserted into the lives of those I protect. You got this one right."

The car halts, and the doors open. He holds up a hand and insists on exiting first, and when we're side by side walking down the hallway, I'm thinking about his emotionless advice. I don't know if he's right or wrong, but I lean toward right. My track record says I'm really wrong about a lot of things that involve my parents. We arrive at my door, and, of course, he's first in, doing a complete search of the place.

When he's cleared my path, he steps back into the hallway. "You're welcome to wait inside with me for Damion."

"Damion would not approve. I'll be right here if you need me."

He's right. Damion wouldn't approve, and while I feel bad for Adam being stuck in the hallway, it's a really good feeling to have Damion on the brink of jealousy. Not that I would intentionally create that in him, nor do I think it's healthy for me to be pleased by such a thing.

I shut the apartment door, with Adam on the other side resting against the hard surface. My gaze sweeps the space I have called home for years now, and there is no part of me that clings to this part of my life, while every part of me has held onto Damion. I'm scared of being hurt by Damion, but I'm far more afraid of never realizing all the possibilities between us.

Damion and I have transitioned from untarnished seven-year-olds in a closet to damaged—some might even say broken—adults about to move in together. It might end up a disaster, but as far as I'm concerned, it will be a beautiful disaster.

# Chapter Thirty-Three

I STAND INSIDE MY small walk-in closet, fretting over which clothes to take with me to Damion's place now versus later, and decide I really need everything. It's not that much, really, and clothes and a few toiletries will get me by just fine. I'm not even sure what else I want to take. My favorite mug, for sure. I'm remarkably unattached to a lot of my things, which says something about me, though I'm not sure what. Or maybe just about my life. I sigh and sit down on the velvet bench I purchased a few months ago, thinking about my decisions over the past few years, and not with pride.

I'd been about to buy an apartment months after the show launch as my way to celebrate the acclaim the show had received; so close, in fact, that I'd picked an adorable place and I was thirty seconds from inking the deal when my mother had come to me, crying. She'd literally cornered me on set, pulled me aside, and turned on hurricane-style waterworks while claiming to have been bullied by debt collectors for my father. I'd been so terrified for her and my father's safety that I'd paid off the seventy-five thousand dollar debt.

*And* I don't know why I think of that memory with the word "claimed" attached at this point. I'm crystal clear on my father's gambling problem. I know the problem is real, but I'm fairly certain I've done nothing to help besides offer a band-aid. I should have demanded he go to therapy—both of them, for that matter.

I've rented this apartment for right at a year, having allowed myself a small upgrade after the show snagged a renewal, that upgrade being a walk-in closet, which is quite the luxury in New York City. The rest of the place is a small box, but I didn't dare go bigger, not when my parents were constantly needing money—ten thousand dollars several times over on top of that seventy-five thousand. What if the next lump sum is six figures? And what happens if I don't give it to them?

There's a shift in the air, and my gaze lifts to find Damion standing in the doorway, looking as Damion always does to me; breathtakingly handsome. My heart leaps at the sight of him, the punch of awareness between us as familiar as it is delicious. His jacket gone, his pressed blue shirt outlining his defined body, his sleeves rolled up to expose his powerful forearms.

I pop to my feet, and he's in front of me instantly, his hands capturing my shoulders, and he drags me to him. "How much money have you given them?" he demands softly.

I blanch, unprepared for the question despite the inevitability of it. "What?" I ask because I can't seem to figure out what else to say.

"This is not how someone of your success level lives, Alana."

There's a pinch in my chest, and my fingers curl at his waist, where they've settled. "You've been here before so I don't know why you're saying this now. And I'm moving in with you, remember?"

"How much?"

Embarrassment washes over me, blood rushing to my cheeks, and I bury my head in his chest. He cups my face and forces my gaze to his burning stare. "Your lack of answer says everything. A lot. And that's why I'm saying this now. Because I've figured out just how used and abused you are. You're selfless and they know it. No more. You are not their bank or an excuse for him to keep on living like this."

It's a command, and while I'm generally hot for every alpha bone in Damion's body, this is personal and painful, and my defenses flare. I twist out of his arms with every intent of placing the stool between us, but he catches my arm and pulls me back to him. "Don't run."

"You don't get to tell me what I do or do not do, Damion. And if living with you means that's how we operate, I'm not moving in with you."

"You know this isn't about me telling you what to do."

"It sounded exactly like that," I snap back.

"Come on, baby," he says, his voice velvety soft. "I'm protecting you."

"By controlling me?"

"Somebody has to snap you to your senses for your own good."

Now he's gone to the wrong place. "And that somebody is you?"

"Consider this an intervention. They need therapy, not another deposit from your bank account."

"You're acting like an asshole. You don't get a say—"

"Really? Is that where you're going with this? I don't get a say, Alana? When do I? When I marry you?"

Emotions explode inside me—years of painful emotions—and I'm embarrassed all over again when I'm already mortified over my parents. The combination is combustible. "Don't throw this damn ring in my face again. But since you did, I don't need to wear it anymore. The farce of an engagement is over. And the whole thing is starting to feel like I'm just pathetic and shouldn't be here." I shove against him and try to push away. God, please just let me end this.

But he won't let that happen. While I've tried to distance myself from him, he's molded me closer, his hand at the back of my head, our mouths close as he says, "If I had my way, I'd officially propose to you right this minute, right here, but I need you to hear what I have to say to you. I need you to know everything. And I'm scared shitless to tell you those things, Alana."

A breath later, his mouth is on mine, his tongue stroking wickedly hot against mine, the truth of his words in his kiss, and I'm drugged with the taste of him and all he has confessed. The instant I sink into the kiss, we're on fire, all over each other, kissing, touching, and hungry for each other in every possible way.

He groans with my hand on his crotch and yanks my skirt up. I end up flat against a wall, and we're both frenzied, struggling with his belt and pants. When he's *finally* free, his thick erection between us, he shoves aside my panties, pulling my leg to his hip and presses inside me. He's hard—so very hard and thick. I gasp with the intensity of him entering me, and he cups my backside, driving deeper. My arms wrap his neck, and his hand slides under my shirt, cupping my breast, deft fingers managing to hold me up and still tease my nipple, thrusting and pulling me down against him.

Never once do I think I'll fall or that he'll drop me. I fell plenty of times when we were kids. He always caught me. He's driving into me, and I'm pressing into him, and the world fades. There is just me and this man, who is everything to me. I am desperate for him, and I can feel his desperation for me. I need more. I have to have more. My orgasm comes hard and fast and without warning. I spasm around him, burying my face in his neck as I gasp with release.

He groans, low, guttural, the intensity of the sound vibrating through me even as he shudders, the warm, wet heat of his release filling me. Seconds pass, and we still, and for a long, few moments, he holds me, his face buried in my neck, his arm tightening around me as if he doesn't want to let me go. And it's a good feeling. I don't want him to let me go.

Slowly, he eases back and stares down at me, his sea-blue eyes stormy, and he says just what I'd thought. "I'm not letting you go. I will *not* let you go."

There's such fierceness to his words, like a man standing in war, holding a sword, and I'm suddenly remembering what he said to me before we got lost in the throes of passion. *I'm scared shitless to tell you those things*, he'd confessed, of whatever he fears his father will tell me first.

"I know whatever it is you don't want to tell me is bad, but I've a lot of practice loving you, Damion. Years are not torn down with words and mistakes."

He draws in a breath and presses his forehead to mine. "Where's the bathroom? I need to get you cleaned up."

"Off the living room," I say, and as he lifts me and carries me that direction, I have this sense that he's holding onto the intimate moment for as long as he possibly can. As if he feels there will never be another.

He doubts we will see that storm in his eyes to the other side, and he has reason. We've always fallen apart.

# Chapter Thirty-Four

"It's barely the size of a small closet," Damion grumbles as we enter my bathroom. "There's nowhere to even sit you down but the damn toilet." He eases me to the ground. "Damn it, Alana."

Embarrassment is perpetual this evening, it seems, as my feet are on the ground but I'm unstable, offering him my back as I grab tissue and tug my skirt down. By the time I've turned around, he's righted his pants, and his attention is fixated on my basic ceramic sink with exposed pipes beneath, before sweeping the remainder of the small space. I'm instantly transported back in time, feeling like the little girl next door whose family lived above their means again, and I start to justify, which translates to I start to ramble. "It's small," I say, "but my closet is big, and it's not a cheap place. This is New York City, and you know—"

"You don't even have a tub," he says, motioning toward the spot where one would be if there was the space, but, of course, there's not. His gaze sharpens on mine. "You love your baths."

I'm fairly certain that anyone who doesn't know Damion as I know him would be stunned at this big, dominant, often hard man, worrying over my baths, or lack thereof. It's somehow odd and right at the same time, and for reasons I can't explain, I feel oh, so naked with him right now, far more so than when my skirt was at my waist. Maybe it's the talk of marriage that we've dared tiptoe yet again, or simply the exposé that could be written on my family drama just this night alone.

He's overwhelmingly present, and I'm overwhelmingly off-kilter. I need out of this tiny room, as he's pointed out, where we might feel slightly less combustible, at least to me. I attempt to walk past him, but he isn't having it. He catches my waist and steps into me, his possessive touch scorching me inside and out.

"Damn it, woman," he murmurs yet again, his tone husky and rough, and he doesn't have to say more. He's worried about my situation. That's what he's telling me. He's worried about me. "I stayed away far too long."

I shove at his unmovable chest. "That entire statement is about you saving me, Damion, and I don't need to be saved."

"It's about being with you, Alana."

"This bathroom and my life," I say, my spine stiff with the reality of my words, "they're both about my decisions, not yours." My fingers curl on the silk of his shirt. "I have to own them."

"Just as I made my decisions that I have to own as well, Alana, but I can't help but think we would have made better ones together."

My shoulders soften, and the breath that I didn't know was lodged in my throat gushes out, and for some silly reason, my eyes pinch. "Yes. I think so, but you're here now, and I'm moving in with you, remember?"

"Are you? Because you threatened to call that off."

"I'm *sorry*," I whisper. "I shouldn't have said that, but I'm just worried about my family taking advantage of you. I don't want my dirty laundry becoming yours. And with me in the spotlight now, that could happen in so many ways."

"Your family is not you. You'll get ratings with a scandal. They'll just get scandal."

"I'm talking about you, Damion."

"Sticks and stones, baby, as you used to say to me when we were kids. The only thing that will break me is losing you again. And as for dirty laundry, as if mine hasn't haunted you your entire life." His expression softens. "Adam told me that you told your mother you'd do anything to protect me."

"Adam has a big mouth, but yes. I did. And I meant it. I will. Always. I need you to know that, Damion."

"You're the only person in my life that I don't pay that I believe has my back. And I have yours."

"I know that, too," I say, swallowing against the dryness in my throat while worry works a number on my heart. "I'm sure Adam told you, but my mom wanted me to come over tonight. She said she and my father had a huge fight. She said it was about his gambling, but I suspect it was about your father."

"Why didn't you go over? Walker would have taken you."

"Because I know you're right about how I've handled them. I need to end this vicious cycle of enabling them. I'm just not sure how. And truth be told, I was really—correction, I *am*—really angry with her over that junk with your father today, but I didn't say anything. I was afraid my attention on the matter would just get back to your father and offer him satisfaction."

"It would have, but at some point, you're also the only person who can jolt your mother back to reality, and that has to be what comes first." His lips press together. "I was thinking about your mother today."

Nerves dance in my belly, telling me this is more than a simple replay of events. "And?" I dare tentatively. I love her. I desperately want her to be safe, but I don't know if I even know who she is anymore. "What about my mother?"

"I worry she's as much a target as you are. Hurting her hurts you, and therefore, me."

It's a brutal truth, and a chill slides down my spine with the validation of my fears. I hug myself. "I thought of the same thing after talking to her tonight. I'm worried she's just a bird in his palm waiting to be crushed."

"As am I. Walker is going to get someone watching them, but there are limits to what they can do without the person's consent."

"I know that. And they're both living on a ledge, dangerously close to a falling off.""

"I wish I could say you're wrong." His lips set, and he considers me a moment before he says, "I handled tonight wrong, Alana, but the way they manipulate you and take advantage of you does not sit well with me." He surprises me then, releasing me and leaning on the sink behind him, considering me and the situation. "Look, baby, I'll empty my bank account for them if that's what you want, but—"

"No. God, no." I erase the space between us; the space I feel as a divide my parents' demands could easily make permanent. "This is exactly what I was afraid of. I do not want them seeing you as a bigger bank, Damion. I'm embarrassed enough that you already bailed them out once. I can't let that happen again."

His hands press to my sides, and his touch is a sweet relief. "You have nothing to be embarrassed about with me," he says. "*Ever.*"

His words matter, they do, and I know he means them, but there is more to this statement than the simple context; a deeper meaning radiating in his tone and in his energy that gives me pause. "You know the same is true with me. And you know what? I don't want you forced into telling me anything. I won't believe anything your father says, anyway. Tell me when you're ready."

His chin lifts, and his gaze with it, and he seems to struggle with words before pinning an unreadable stare on me. "Get dressed. I want you out of this place. I want you home with me, but I also know you well enough to know we need to go see your mother."

"No, I'm okay," I say quickly. "I told her no."

"And I'm telling you yes. Alana, if something happens to either of them, you will never forgive yourself. We'll go by there on the way home, and I can stay in the car or go up with you."

I should move. I should be all-in with where this is headed, but my mind rejects his plan and does so with certainty. Just moments before, he shut me down when I told him he had nothing to be embarrassed about with me, shut me down cold with a change of topic. That's what this is: him using my mother to shift the attention off of himself and what he feels is some failure I won't be able to live with, and back to me.

And I can't let that happen.

I *won't* let that happen.

I wrap my arms around him, tilt my chin up, and meet his shuttered stare. "I know everything I need to know about you, Damion. So, I repeat, I won't believe anything your father says to me. No matter *what* he says to me. Tell me your truth when you're ready, Damion, and not a moment sooner."

His expression transforms into dark lines and shadows, his lashes lowering, seconds ticking by before he says, "The problem is, I'll never be ready, Alana."

"Then don't tell me."

"I *have* to tell you, and not because of my father. Because I don't want us to be like our parents. Because you need to know who you're spending your life with. I just hoped to have time to let you see that I'm still me, I'm still the man you've always known, before I did. But that bastard is going to take that from me and us."

"Don't let him, Damion. Don't allow him to make you feel pressured. We're okay, I promise you. But just because I think you need to hear it, I already know you're the same man." I press my hand to his heart. "I know what you are inside. I know all kinds of things about you, like how you know I love my baths. And I love who you are."

"I love you, too, baby, and, unfortunately, he's always known that, too." He strokes my hair. "Let's go see your mother."

"No," I say firmly. "I told my mother I'm not coming over, and it's the first time I've ever drawn a line in the sand, Damion. I needed to draw that line, and you did that for me. You made me stronger just by being in my life. And we need this night, the night I move in with you, to be about us."

"Are you sure? Because we can just do a quick stop."

"There is no 'quick' when my mother is in drama mode. I want to go home to *our* home together. And for the record, I'm your ride or die. I'd bury a body for you."

It's a common saying, but it hits a nerve quite obviously. Torment rips through his stare, and then he's back to staring at the ceiling, and my heart twists with uncertainty. What did I say wrong? "Damion," I whisper, compelling him to look at me, and the torment of moments before is not gone. It's oh, so present, and it crashes into me in hot, rolling waves. "You might just have to, Alana," he says, his voice deep and raspy, but he doesn't give me time to reply.

He pushes off the sink and laces his fingers with mine. "Let's pack you up and, as you said, *go home*."

I want to say more. I want to turn back time and take back my silly statement, but I cannot. And there is nothing I can do right now to make this right—to make him whole and us stronger—but go home with him.

# Chapter Thirty-Five

Damion calls Adam into the room, and before I know it, the two of them go to work moving my things, and a mere fifteen minutes later, my clothes are packed into the SUV. While they make trips downstairs, I toss things into boxes. I'm overpacking when I'd planned to keep this simple and let the movers do the rest, but I feel a deep-rooted need to make this move feel official for both of us.

I need Damion to know this is official and that I'm all-in.

When I'm finally done packing all I can take with me tonight, I debate my furniture. Should I store it or sell it? I hate the warning zipping through me, telling me to keep it handy. *That's not all-in*, I chide myself. I'll sell it, end of topic. Decision made, I hunt for my cellphone, which leads me to the closet, where I find it on the stool. I snatch it up to find four missed calls from my mother and a slew of text messages. I sink onto the stool with the weight of the mental and emotional exhaustion my family drama has created.

I draw a hard-earned breath and read the messages.

Number one: *Damion ripped your heart out when you were a teen. You think he won't do it again? You're the flavor of the month, and what happens when you piss him off and he ends your show?*

Number Two: *Answer my calls! I'm your mother!*

Number Three: *I know things about Damion you need to know.*

My hand presses to my belly. Oh God. This is it. This is how Damion's father is using my mother. He's going to have her spill the dirty laundry Damion's certain his father will use against him. Suddenly, my strong instinct to stay away from her tonight makes sense. I'd sensed this on that call. I'd known she'd work against me and Damion.

I force myself to read her final message: *I'm coming over. We're going to talk, and you WILL listen to me.* My heart lurches, and I eye the time. Thirty minutes ago. I launch myself to my feet and try to call her, but land in her voicemail. It's right then that I hear, "Damion. Oh my. You're here."

Oh no. *Oh God.*

At the sound of my mother's voice, I all but torpedo out of the closet and through the bedroom. I enter the living room to find Damion sitting on the arm of my couch, my mother all but in his face. She's of petite stature, shorter than me by an inch, attractive, and her large, rather righteous personality is in full flex. Damion, on the other hand, is alpha dominance personified, and yet he's backed away, given her respect and space, intentionally chosen not to tower over her. He grew up around her and offered her respect; he's extending that to her now because she's my mom. We all have history, and it means the world to me.

I'm just not sure she deserves it.

"Why didn't you just stay in Europe?" my mother demands of Damion.

"Because Alana was here," he says simply.

"Oh, please," she says, rolling her eyes. "You're here for your father's empire, not my daughter, and somehow, someway, she's part of your strategy to rule your father's world. I will not see her hurt."

"The way you try and rule mine," I demand, bitterness lacing and settling heavily in my belly, so much bitterness.

She whirls on me. "I do not, and don't let him turn you against me."

"Damion has never said one bad word about you. Just the opposite."

Her spine straightens, and her neck stretches. "We need to talk."

"It would not be in your best interest that we talk right now," I say. "I need some space. I've needed it for a long time. Damion, I'm ready."

He pushes to his feet. "Why don't I give you a few? I'll be outside the door." There's a push to his words, as if he's compelling me to take the time and talk to my mother; a grace she doesn't deserve, but he's offering her.

My lips press together, and emotion wells in my chest, but I give him a short nod. He studies me a moment, as if assessing my state of mind, warmth in his eyes and a promise that he's with me all the way. The bond between us is familiar and calming, right in ways nothing else has ever been in my life.

He tears his gaze from mine, reluctance in the act, but he moves swiftly toward the door, exiting and leaving my mother alone with me. The minute the door shuts, I pounce. "You do realize he paid off a six-figure debt for you and dad."

"And left me indebted to his father. It's all a game with that family, a power play."

"You seem pretty willing and ready for his father. I think you want the comfort of his money and the prestige of being on his arm."

"It's not true."

"He took you to Damion's attorney's office to send Damion a message. You have to know that."

"And what message would that be?"

"That he's close to me. That he will hurt me if Damion doesn't back off. That he can hurt you to hurt me. You're a target, and he will destroy you and me, and you're just letting it happen."

"No. No, that's not true."

"You're cheating on Dad, and you're defending the man you're cheating with."

"I'm protecting your father." She breathes out a shaky breath. "We borrowed more money. Your dad told me just to do what I had to do." She bursts into tears.

I wait for the compassion to kick in, for my need to hug her and love her to win me over, but it doesn't happen. It's as if a switch has flipped, and I'm simply immune to the same ol' same ol'. And the idea that my father would excuse her sleeping with Damion's father is illogical. He tried to ruin Damion's father. He lost his mind over this very topic. "Why didn't I know about this?" I ask, and even to me, my voice sounds cold and distant.

She sobs and swipes at her eyes. "Because I knew you were at your limit, and I felt like I was a horrid mother for laying this on you."

"So, sleeping around on Dad makes you a great mother?" I demand, stunned that the woman who truly was an amazing parent as I grew up has become what she is now, and I don't even know how to label that transition. "Dad needs to go into rehab, and I'm going to talk to him about it. I'll pay for it, but I will not pay off any more debt."

"He'll never go."

My throat is thick with the words I've wanted to speak for months that I dread speaking but know I must. "I looked up a rehab in France. Actually, I talked to them. They're an amazing place that specializes in addicts and those who enable them. I'll send you both there for a month. It will be good for you both. You have to break this cycle."

She stares at me for several long beats and then laughs a choked laugh that sounds almost hysterical before she turns on her heels and simply walks out of the door. I'm left gaping and stunned and so very confused. My hand presses to my belly, where an uncomfortable sensation has formed. What is happening? How have I lost my family this much?

My lashes lower, and suddenly Damion is in front of me, his warm hands on my face, when I never even heard him enter the apartment. "What happened?"

"I don't want to talk about it right now," I say. "I mean, I will, just not this second." My fingers catch on the silk of his shirt, and I remember so many times in my young life when he was there for me, just as he is now, and I know where I want to be and what I want to do. "Can we just…go home?"

His eyes are now as warm as his hands. "Yeah, baby. Let's go home."

# Chapter Thirty-Six

## Damion

I know Alana, and she's barely holding it together, bleeding inside over her parents, and I'm bleeding with her.

No one knows how the destruction of what you call family can rip you apart like I do. Exactly why I hate to tell her what awaits us downstairs. I capture her waist and steady her, aware that she's on unsteady ground. "We have an audience downstairs. The press found us."

"No," she whispers, pressing her hands to her face for a brief moment. "This is nuts. I've never had this kind of attention."

"It's us together," I say. "A fascination that won't last. We just have to ride out the storm."

"What about your board and all you have pending? Doesn't this look like a circus?"

"It's irrelevant." I pull my phone from my pocket, and in an effort to draw her further from her mother's visit, I hold it out to her. "But attention-grabbing. Mary texted."

She accepts the phone and stares down at the newest photo of us together that's all over the internet before reading it out loud. "Treat her better than you're treating me." She hands me the phone. "Can I call her?"

"I called her. I assured her I'm treating you like a princess."

"And her?"

"The queen she wants to be. I told her we'd have breakfast with her Sunday morning to talk about the future."

"Isn't that premature when you haven't had the board meeting? Or did something happen I don't know about?"

I slide her hair behind her ear. "Plenty is happening, but we can talk about it at home tonight...or not. We can always save it for tomorrow."

She surprises me by breaking into a charming, spontaneous smile, and damn, she's beautiful—so fucking beautiful. "Yes. Home."

I think I forgot how to smile this past decade without her, but I do so now, and do so with the ease of a man far more comfortable in her presence than I am without her.

I lace her fingers with mine, guiding her toward the door, and once we're there, I say, "Any last-minute things you need to grab?"

"I took way more than I meant to. Honestly, my lease has almost a year left on it. There isn't even a rush to get a mover over here."

"I want to give the damn thing away so you can't come back," I say, "but I'll add a more civilized option so you won't get mad at me. We can pay it off and sell what you don't want to keep, if you want."

She laughs, pushes to her toes, and kisses my cheek. I catch her around the waist and hold her to me, just like I'm going to do for the rest of her life. "I prepaid for my lease," she informs me. "I was ah—" She pushes out of my hold, her gaze averted as she adds, "I didn't want to have anything put me in a bad spot."

She means her parents, and I swear I want to go to her father and throttle him for allowing all of what has happened. The root of the poison starts with him.

"Maybe I can let someone use it," she muses, "though I'm not sure who."

"We'll figure it out," I say, capturing her hand and guiding her back to my side. "Let's really go this time." She nods eagerly, and I open the door.

We step into the hallway, where Adam pushes off the wall, on ready. I incline my chin, and Adam speaks into his earpiece. "On our way down." He moves ahead of us and punches the elevator call button.

Once the doors open, he checks the car and then motions us forward. I slide my arm around Alana's shoulders, and we enter the car. Once we're sealed inside, she leans forward to eye Adam. "You have a big mouth."

His brows lift. "Do I?"

She rotates out of my arms to face him. "You cannot follow me around if I feel like you're going to repeat everything I say to Damion. And don't say it's your job. Telling him I said I'd do anything to protect him is not about my safety."

I step between them, hands on her shoulders, and stare down at her. "It is about your safety, because that's what your mother is going to tell my father. And everything that gets to my father frames his next action."

"Then I probably screwed us all. I told my mother she's made herself a target and me with her."

I give her shoulders a gentle squeeze. "You said nothing but the obvious. Give Adam a break. He's protecting you and doing a damn good job of it."

Her lashes lower, and she nods. The elevator opens, and she whispers, "I'm sorry. I just—" Her eyes meet mine. "I feel like the entire world is watching me, really us, and I just have this sense it's all going to blow up in our faces."

She's talking about her family scandal, which is nothing compared to mine. And while I'd been certain I needed to pull off the band-aid and tell her everything tonight, I'm not sure if I should bury her in the burden all at once or wait. I want to wait, and it would be easy to justify doing so, but I need to think and force objectivity. Either way, I can't get her home with me fast enough.

The door starts to buzz, and I glance over my shoulder to realize Adam's holding it open. I twine the fingers of one of Alana's hands in mine. "You ready for this?" I ask, speaking of the crowds we've been promised outside.

"As ready as I'll ever be," she says, and the words punch me in the gut.

She is as ready as she ever will be for any of this because she'll never be ready for what I have to tell her. We approach the lobby door, and there's a team waiting on us. Kelvin exits before us, and Adam motions for us to follow, with him at our rear. A wave of protectiveness overcomes me, and I pull Alana close, sheltering her, some part of me afraid I can never protect her from what's coming. Because it is; something big and bad is coming, and there's no running. We have to stand and face it head-on.

Cameras flash, and our names are shouted, but finally we end up in the back of the SUV, Adam across from us, the door locked, and the vehicle moving. "I'm sorry, Adam," Alana says. "I'm kind of a mess right now. I know—"

"I get it," he says, shortening her plea for forgiveness with understanding. "It's not easy to have me around."

"It's not you, though," she says. "You've been great."

"I'm only as great as the next moment we're in together. But I'll be careful to respect your privacy."

My cellphone buzzes with a text message, and I swear a ball of dread forms in my gut for no explainable reason. I slip it from my pocket to find a message from my mother: *911.* It's the code she promised to use if my father contacted her. *And fuck him.* That's my mother. Always the fiercest of them all.

Another message pings, and this one is from my father: *Every beast has horns and talons. Do you really want to see mine? Last chance to make this right. Cash out and walk away. Or else.*

Anger bubbles inside me. He's fucking threatening Alana, and I'm at my limit. I reply with: *You think she makes me weak. You're wrong. The wrath I will regin down on you if you touch her is unfathomable. Anything you think I will hold back, I will not.*

*Ah, son,* he replies. *When you talk like that, you make me proud, but there is a softness inside you that neither of us can deny. You are no match for me.*

*As the famous saying goes,* I reply, *arrogance is the surest path to failure.*

And because he can't allow me the last word, he concludes with: *We'll see.*

Seconds tick by, adrenaline pouring through my veins, before I pull up Caleb's number and text: *I need to see you.*

He answers immediately: *When?*

*This weekend. I'll let you know, but acting on my father's behalf is not in your best interest.*

*I'll wait to hear from you on all points*, he replies, and I slide my phone back in my pocket to find Alana staring at me, her eyes wide and worried.

"What just happened?" she asks softly.

"Nothing that matters tonight."

"But it matters?" she presses.

"Maybe," I say, not willing to be pushed into saying more—not here and now, at least. I need to think about where I'm headed with that message to Caleb and just how dirty I'm willing to get.

The vehicle pulls up at the rear of my apartment, which I assume means the front is a mass of reporters. "We're clear for entry," Adam informs me as if reading my mind. He exits the rear door, does whatever he does, and then leans inside again. "Let's move."

I kiss Alana's hand. "Home sweet home, baby." I soften my voice. "Let's go upstairs." I don't give her the chance to argue. I exit the vehicle and take her with me with no intent of allowing my father to ruin the first night Alana calls my home her home.

# Chapter Thirty-Seven

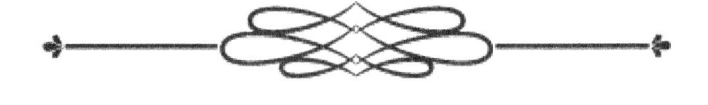

## *Alana*

The trip inside the building that is my new home is as easy as a summer breeze offering relief from the burning hot sun—or, in our case, the press. But there is little to offer relief from the battle raging around us. I don't know who Damion was texting with on the ride here, but I know the hard set of his jaw and the sharpness of his eyes well enough to be certain the content was about his father.

The control freak in me that studied into the wee hours to ensure I had perfect grades craves information and wants to demand he spill the goods. But as he folds his arm around me and ushers me into the elevator, the warmth of his touch is a welcome distraction from the world outside. I'm not sure I want to risk cooling the heat between us for what will most certainly strike a foreboding tone.

Once we're inside the car, Adam joins us, and it's him, not Damion, who punches in our destination. Damion and I face forward, but there's a thick layer of awareness between us, an intimacy that isn't about sex as much as it is about me going home with him, and not to his home, but ours. I am warm inside and out and a tad bit nervous, which is really quite ridiculous. This is Damion, who I have known all my life and who I love more than life. Why would I be nervous about the launch of our life together? Especially when I believe the root of who we are began decades before this night.

My mind travels to that kiss in the closet when we were seven, then the kiss at my front door before he left for college, and somehow, I detour to my mother. Of course, after her explosion in my apartment, it's really no surprise, but the way she treated Damion and the things she said don't even align with the way she's felt about him most of our lives. Even after I'd cried that day he'd kissed me on my porch, after I'd declared the end of me and Damion, my mother had defended him. She'd told me we were young, and if it was meant to be, we'd find each other again. And we have, and that matters. It matters so very much, and yet she didn't share my joy with me today. She tried to destroy the man I love, tried to destroy *us*, me and Damion, and for what? Or rather, who?

His father? Who she's having an affair with?

My mind flashes back to the past...

Damion and I had both been seventeen, or maybe he'd just turned eighteen. We'd hit the movies together and saw the new Hunger Games movie, an easy thing to do when my mother and his girlfriend had been out with friends, separately, of course, while my father was working late. Damion's parents never really questioned where he was or what he was doing, and I swear my mother fretted over him more than they did.

She was good to him then but she was horrible to him tonight.

I return to the memory.

We'd had fun that night, but then we always did, laughing together and trying to catch popcorn in our mouths, but I'd been acutely aware of how soon he'd leave for college. So was he. It was there between us, a living, breathing temptation, and a few times I think he'd been close to kissing me, but he *had a girlfriend*. Another reality I'd been acutely aware of pretty much every second I was with him.

We'd stopped by a diner on the way home, and to our shock, we'd found my mother and his father together. I'd wanted to approach the table, but Damion had caught my arm. I sink back into that moment, reliving it:

*"No," he insists. "We don't know what this is." He captures my hand and all but drags me out of the joint.*

*The instant we're outside, out of view of the diner windows, I whirl on him, "What are you suggesting is going on between them?"*

*"We don't know, Alana," he bites out, his hands settling on his hips.*

*"You think they're having an affair? My mother does not like your father. She calls him arrogant."*

*"You call me arrogant," he reminds me.*

*"You are arrogant, Damion West."*

*"And yet you're out with me tonight."*

*"As a friend."*

*"Right," he bites out. "As a friend." He scrubs his jaw and then offers me a view of his broad shoulders as he walks away.*

I blink after him, stunned for a few beats, before I catch up with him, confusion setting my thoughts into a spin. "Why are you angry at me?"

"I'm not angry at you, Alana," he snaps, but he doesn't look at me.

I catch his arm, and he halts, piercing me with sharp eyes. "What are you trying to do right now?"

"What do you mean?" I whisper, that confusion leaving me unsteady.

"What do you think touching me achieves?"

"What? Are you thinking someone will think we're together?"

"Everyone but us thinks we're together, Alana. Wake up." He starts walking again.

I double-step and catch up to him again, but I don't speak this time, and I certainly don't touch him. The three-block walk was the most uncomfortable few minutes I've ever shared with Damion that didn't involve one of his girlfriends, none of who thought me and Damion were together. I want to say that, but it just doesn't feel right.

When we finally arrive at my house, he rotates to face me. "Do not bring up seeing them together. It's our secret. Understand?"

"Understand?" I ask incredulously. "Don't talk to me like that."

He grabs my arm and pulls me close—so very close that I can smell him and feel his hard body. "Our secret, Alana."

My body tingles with the way our thighs touch, with the impact of this intimacy after hours of being alone with him, wishing he'd kiss me, knowing it would be wrong.

"Say it," he presses.

"Our secret," I agree.

He studies me several beats, seeming to weigh my commitment to that vow, before he sets me away from him. "I need to go before I do something we both regret." He rotates on his heels and leaves me standing on my front lawn.

I blink back to the present just as the elevator doors open on our floor, and there is acid bubbling in my belly. The history between me and Damion is a river that runs wild and deep. What if my mother's history with his father runs just as wild and deep? What if every tear she has shed in front of me was all a show? What if she wants to be with Damion's father?

What else would she do for that man?

The problem is, I have no answer. I don't even know who she is anymore.

Adam steps out of the car, checks the hallway, and then motions for me and Damion to follow, only to point to a spot beside the door where he intends for us to wait. The very idea that we have to be concerned about someone waiting on us inside turns the warmth of moments before into discomfort. What do they know that I do not? Damion's behind me now, his hands on my shoulders as he turns me to face him.

"Relax, baby. He's just being vigilant."

"What don't I know, Damion?"

"My father as well as I do."

I think of his reaction in the diner that night, so many years ago. He knows his father. He knew what was happening between him and my mother wasn't innocent. A chill runs down my spine as I think of those flowers that we have yet to talk about and the card attached: *What I give, I can take away.*

I dig in my pocket, pull out that note, and hand it to Damion. Damion stares down at it and then lifts his gaze to mine. His expression is indecipherable, but his jaw is a band of muscle, his body next to mine is steel. "I know Adam told you about this."

"He did."

"What does he think he gave me?"

"He's arrogant enough to believe he allows those around him to live and thrive. Therefore, he's God. He gives those around him the very breath they breathe."

A chill runs down my spine. "And he can take it away," I whisper.

"Yes, baby. That's what I've been telling you. He doesn't just believe he can. He believes it's his right."

# Chapter Thirty-Eight

I want to ask Damion so many things right now.

Does he know if they were having an affair way back then? Does she hate him because he knows things I do not that he might tell me? And I want to tell him I'm sorry for how she treated him, but the elevator dings to our right. I'm so very on edge that I whip around to watch Kelvin step out with a load of my things in his arms. Adam exits the apartment, and the moment of truth with Damion is lost.

Adam clears us to enter the apartment, and Damion catches me to him and kisses me. "We'll talk. We have a lifetime to sort out the details. Let's get you settled and them out of here."

A lifetime.

Those words rush through me, as confusing and sweet as rain on a scorching hot sunny day. But maybe they are not all that confusing at all. We have known each other a lifetime. We're connected. There is nothing that can erase that bond, and I shove the naysaying in my mind away, refusing to give it a voice.

I push to my toes and kiss him. "Yes. Let's get me moved in."

His hand presses warmly, possessively, on my lower back, and he murmurs, "I love you, Alana. Don't ever forget that." The thundering of his heart beneath my palm drives home the promise of a storm before us in that proclamation.

"I love you, too. And don't ever forget that."

He kisses me, a long stroke of tongue, before catching my hand in his and leading me toward the door. A few minutes later, I'm in his—no, our—enormous closet organizing my clothes while the sound of male voices lift, followed by laughter, Damion's laughter, and it's sweet music to my ears. Too many years passed without that sound in my life, without him in my life.

Once I've lined up my clothes, I hurry into the bathroom and claim a few spots as my own, hoping Damion doesn't mind. It's all so surreal. When I'm finally done, I step into the closet again and just stare at my clothes opposite Damion's clothes. I walk to the rows of suits and run my hand over the finely woven fabric.

It's then that I realize the apartment is silent, and I wonder if I'm alone. Unease fills me, and I exit the closet, walk through the bedroom, and pause in the doorway between it and the living room. I find Damion in one of two leather chairs facing the window that appear to be new, his jacket gone, his sleeves rolled up to the elbow and displaying his powerful forearms.

He downs the contents of a glass and reaches for the bottle on a table next to him, pouring amber liquid, allowing it to slosh around the ice. It's only then that I recognize the familiar beauty of a classical violin, the same music he'd favored as an older teen, and not during happy times. This was how he escaped the hell of his many battles with his father—brutal battles at times. Damion would be left bruised and bloody inside, if not outside, feeling as if he wasn't good enough for his father. As if he wasn't living life as his father demanded and expected. This music was always a sign of dark times for Damion.

Damion leans back in his chair and tilts his head skyward, the glass resting in his hand, his energy a heavy pulse. Something has happened—something that has deeply upset him—and my gut knots with this absolute certainty. And just as I didn't hesitate to go to him during his turbulent times in the past, I won't now, either.

Decision made, I cross the room, confirming the pair of chairs and the small table to be new and, I suspect, for us to share the view. This touches me deeply, and I settle on my knees in front of him, my hands on his knee next to me.

There's a flex of muscle beneath my palm and his head lifts, dark eyes meeting mine, a punch of his torment stealing my breath, but somehow, I offer a raspy, "Hi."

He downs the contents of his glass again, discarding it as he sets it next to the bottle, before he leans close and catches a strand of my hair. "Hi," he says softly. "All settled?" There's a gentleness to his tone that defies the intensity of his mood.

"I am," I say, "but obviously you are not."

"You being here with me, Alana, is everything."

It's not an answer. In fact, it's the avoidance of an answer. "But it doesn't make all the chaos around us go away, now does it?" I ask. "There's a reason you're out here alone."

"Waiting on you, baby. That's all. Just waiting on you."

"And raking yourself over the coals because your father did as well. Did you think I'd forget your way of dealing with him or this music?"

His lips lift; more of that tenderness I feel in him tonight in the curve of his mouth, but it can't break through the darkness of his mood. "Of course you didn't," he says softly, his fingers trailing over my jaw. "Do you know how many times since I bought this apartment a few months ago that I stood at this window, wishing you were here?"

I want to push him to tell me what happened with his father, but I can sense that he doesn't want to talk. He will, I know he will, but he has a process with his father and with all challenges, and I have to give him time to process. "I'm here now," I murmur. "And I wouldn't be anywhere but here."

He stands and takes me with him, his hand sliding under my hair and pressing warmly to my neck. "I don't want you to be anywhere but here, Alana. I should never have stayed away this long. I should have ended this and done so decisively, but I'm going to now. Walker is here. They'll stay with you, but I have to go out for a little while—"

"No," I say, my heart leaping and my fingers curling at his sides around his shirt. "No, you will not. We agreed that tonight—"

"I'm making sure we have many more nights," he vows, his mouth slanting over my mouth, tongue stroking deep. And just that easily, I'm drowning in all things Damion West; in the taste of him, the musky male scent of him fills me up and slides inside the emptiness that was me without him. I'd convinced myself so many times in my life that I didn't need him, but I do. I need him with every part of me, and too easily I've seen how we fall apart.

The very thought has me pushing on his chest, shoving him back, and not gently. He sits in the chair, and I climb right on top of him, straddling him, my hands planting on his shoulders. "He pushed your buttons, Damion. And every time he does, you react fast and hard, and it's the only time I've seen you act rashly. He knows that, too. Wait to do whatever you plan to do. Wait until morning."

His hands settle warmly on my waist; his touch is possessive and all-consuming. The heat between us is downright combustible, but his lashes sweep low on his cheeks and there is a tic in his jaw. "Damion," I press, my hand to his jaw, rough stubble against my delicate skin, but it is the only part of me that is delicate right now. He needs to hear me. "Please look at me."

He presses his hand to mine, curls it into his, easing it between us. His blue eyes are a mix of tenderness and steel that tells me he's already made up his mind. "We've waited a lifetime for this night."

"We have," he says, with such certainty in his voice that it's as if I've made his point for him.

"What does that even mean?" I ask, certain that it reaches beyond the obvious.

"We waited too long, Alana. *I* waited too long to come for you, and the reason I waited was because I submit to him when I submit to no one. That's what he expects of me. More of the same." He stands up and takes me with him, his hands on my face, tilting my gaze to his. "You woke me up. This has gone on too long." His thumb strokes my cheek. "Trust me, baby. I need to take action. I'm clearing that path I promised you I'd clear. So you can marry me."

His mouth closes over mine, his tongue sliding deep, and I moan with the taste of man and whiskey, a swell of emotion overwhelming me. I want to push away from him and force him to talk to me. I want to drag his hands to my body and distract him from his father's head games, but I never get the chance to do either.

He tears his mouth from mine, his breath warm and heavy on my lips, mine all but coming out in pants. "I'll try not to be late. Lock up behind me." He sets me away from him, and before I can blink, he's around the chairs and headed for the door, grabbing his jacket at the door and turning to me. "Come lock up."

I snap out of my stunned state and rush that direction, but he doesn't wait for me. He exits the apartment. Once I'm at the door, I want to open it. I want to go after him, but I know it's too late. He's gone.

# Chapter Thirty-Nine

## *Damion*

Control is a king's gold, my father has always told me, and control has been his for far too long. Leaving Alana tonight is the last thing I want to do, but it's necessary. My father has to be dealt with, and until that happens, she'll never be safe.

I exit the elevator at the lobby, where Adam waits on me. He offers me a nod and steps into the car, on his way to our floor, where he will closely guard the apartment and Alana. I trust him, which is not something I say of many people I've recently met, or even known for a lifetime, for that matter. But Blake doesn't steer me wrong. He chooses his men closely, and it shows. He has morals. They do, too. It's a unique perspective on living if you judge the world by those who gather and occupy mine.

I cross the lobby with measured steps and exit to a chilly night, where an SUV is waiting on me in front of the building, ready to deliver me to my meeting with Caleb. Once inside the backseat, I find Savage waiting for me on the seat across from me. He's a big man, at least six-three, with a scar down his cheek and, based on the one time I met him before, a stupid sense of humor that somehow works for him when it would for no other.

There's nothing comical about him at the moment, though; his jaw set hard, his eyes sharp. He tosses a file on the seat next to me. "Before we leave, you need to look inside. That's the many horrors that call Caleb a monster, not a man, and you don't trust monsters."

I don't reach for the file. "Were you once a killer just like him?"

"Not just like him," he says without hesitation. "I worked for a man I believed to be honorable, and believed I killed the enemies of this country. But what you need to know about becoming a contract killer is how easily you begin to kill. How removed from humanity you become."

"Then what makes you different from him?"

"Aside from the reason I took the jobs I executed, which was not money," he holds up his hand and indicates his wedding ring, "she does. And thank fuck I met her before I went off to war, or I might have become just like him. And for the record, the reason I trusted the man I worked for was not just his medals and rank. He was her father, and my father was worse. So I get fucked up families and fucked up fathers, and I'm telling you right now: use Caleb for information you most likely won't get from him, but that's it. One of us needs to put a bullet in his head, and I'll do it without a blink. I won't wake up guilty over it tomorrow."

"You misjudge me if you think I'd feel guilty about killing a man who'd easily take cash to kill my woman. But he feels some sort of connection to me that I would not call loyalty or a compliment. It simply exists. I've never figured it out, but I'm willing to use it."

"How?" he asks.

"Information. Which means you can't be with me."

"That's a mistake," he replies. "Because whatever you think you know about him, I know more. And he'll know I know more. A killer knows a killer when he looks them in the eye." He leans in closer and meets my stare. "I'm looking into your eyes. You are not a killer. Don't kid yourself into thinking otherwise. He doesn't respect you, not the way you need him to respect you, not unless you come with me."

"So, you want him to respect you?" I bite out.

"Bringing me gets you respect. You don't need to be the guy who'll pull the trigger. You just need to be smart enough to hire the guy who will. That's your respect."

That comment punches and then spirals to a pit in my soul where all things my father live and just won't die. Everything he suggests is a little too like my father for my comfort. I became a little too like my father for my liking, most certainly Alana's, but she's been a target all her life because of me.

She deserves freedom from my family.

She deserves to have me fight for her.

"Let's go see Caleb," I say, and I don't reach for the file.

I know far more about Caleb than Savage believes I do.

And I'm not sure Caleb sees anything but my father's son when he looks at me.

Which makes me a killer, even if not the kind Savage calls familiar.

# Chapter Forty

Caleb chooses our meeting location, a two-level hole in the wall restaurant and bar, which in New York City, is eighty percent of the establishments, and usually not a testament to the caliber of the company it keeps. In this case, *it is*. The joint is smokey, and loud upstairs, and smokey and dirty downstairs. To add to the ambience of it all, a few seedy looking characters lurk about, adding to my certainty that this is not a place my father would ever be seen, which I assume to be the point.

With Savage by my side, we weave our way through the rectangular space, sidestepping wooden tables with barstools, both of us in silent agreement that we're headed downstairs. The stairwell is to the right and made for one, and neither me nor Savage are small people. We share a look and I go first, with him at my back, a little too close if you ask me, but he's on a mission to be present and account for, and charging toward that goal, even if he's forced to go second. I reach the worn hardwood below to find a cluster of jean clad men shooting pool around a beat-up table, but there is no sign of Caleb.

My gaze lifts to the bar in the left corner, and to the right of it, there's a hallway.

Savage, already by my side, says, "He'll be back there," he glances over at me. "I would."

In other words, it's a kill spot, and Caleb's a killer and a money man. I'm not immune to the idea that he might have me on his hitlist. Savage as my sidekick is looking smarter by the minute as is the weapon tucked by my side.

"And yes," Savage replies, as if I've asked a question. "I'm armed and dangerous."

Of that, I have no doubt.

"Let's get this over with," I say.

He winks at me like a fool, but somehow, it's this part of him, the ability to joke in the face of danger, that makes him so damn lethal.

I start walking, and again step in front of Savage as we single file our way toward those back rooms. Once we're in the small hallway, there's room for two, and Savage steps to my side yet again. We end up cutting right into a surprisingly large room with low as hell ceilings and I'm reminded of what Savage said earlier.

*He'll be there. I would be.*

Or whatever the fuck he said.

It's a secluded spot that might as well be a dark alley.

Never in my decades of knowing Caleb have I considered him my future hitman, but I do now. I bring the room into full view with only one person present. Caleb sits at a long wooden table, a bottle of whiskey and two glasses in front of him, as if he plans to give me a reason to drink.

Two long tables stand between us and him. I walk around them and join Caleb. He stands and faces me, ignoring Savage. "Who the fuck is he?"

"I be Savage," Savage says. "I kill people." He laughs. "Sounds like fun, right?"

Caleb's gaze shifts to Savage and the two men stare each other down for so fucking long, I sit down and fill my glass. When the pair of them decide to join me, Savage downs the contents of Caleb's glass and says, "Nice of you to provide treats." He refills the glass. "Just so you know, if you kill Damion or Alana, I'm your Huckleberry. Should you do so, Damion offered to pay me a shit ton of money to kill you, but I declined. I love killing one of *you*. I'll do it for free."

I almost laugh at Savage, for no good reason. This isn't funny. It's not even close to funny but it's just stupid ridiculous. Even by my standards, having grown up with my mother, It's like something out of a movie not real life. Caleb's gaze is steel locked on Savage's face before it shifts sharply to me. "What is this?"

"We both know your ultimate loyalty lies with my father."

He doesn't so much as blink. "I'd tell you to give me a reason to be loyal to you, but you can't win this, Damion. Therefore, I can't win with you." He taps the glass. "Drink it. You're about to need it."

"Say what you have to say," I snap.

"All right. Let's get right to it, no lube or booze. He's got a bloody good plan. He's fucking Alana's mother for a reason. You can let your mind go wild and imagine where I'm going with this. I won't fill in the blanks, but if anything he plans goes wrong I'm responsible. There's a price on my head. It's all paid for. It's all done. There's only one way to stop it."

I bark out laughter. "Let me guess. Sell my stock to him."

"Exactly," he says, and he grabs the glass Savage has just filled and downs it. "Exactly." His eyes meet Savages. "Unless Savage here wants to help me kill off all the contract killers in the world, of which there are more than you might think, I find myself in a quandary." He sets the glass down and looks at me. "I either finish the job he's put before me, or I could be the next one to die."

"Kill or be killed," Savage replies dryly. "I don't believe for a minute you're operating on fear or threats. Anyone of our caliber welcomes another one of us to come at them. I damn sure do. Why do you think I'm here right now?" My cellphone buzzes with a text and Savage says, "You'll want to read that message, Damion" to me, obviously wearing an earbud or mic, and already in the know.

Curiosity that matches mine sparks in Caleb's eyes and I remove my phone from my pocket and read the message from Blake: *Caleb has a daughter. She's two. He met her mother, Sara, while she worked for your father, and he shipped her off to an island in Hawaii where she changed her name. They don't speak. Word is that she found out what he does for a living, really does, and wanted nothing to do with him. I'd say he's too cold to care, but he keeps tabs on them. He paid to move her and change her name. Those actions say you will know what he wants no one to know. Show him this photo. It was taken today.*

A photo of a pretty little brunette girl and a mother fill my screen.

Of course, there's a moral question to what I've been offered for personal use, but I won't kill his daughter and neither will Walker Security. He'll know this. Just as I know he *will* kill Alana. I use the gift I've been given in the only way it works in this situation and set the phone in front of Caleb. "Does my father know about them?"

Caleb eyes the phone, heavy seconds ticking by, his expression unreadable but there is a pulse to his energy, a darkening of his mood. When his eyes meet mine, he says, "This changes nothing. He's already set actions in motion."

"There's a way to stop this," I say, and tap the photo, reminding him what's at stake. "If you think I won't tell him, you're wrong. Alana is a game changer for me. Telling him pits you against him and links your survival, your daughter's survival, and Alana's survival together."

His eyes glint. "It also pits you against me. And if you think we have some bond that means I won't kill you myself for no reason other than you pissed me off, you're wrong."

"I feel we've forgotten I'm here," Savage interjects. "And as I hear all that you are saying Caleb, you're just lighting me up inside with excitement. I get to kill you." He rubs his hands together. "Let's do it."

"That wedding ring says you have a reason to stay the fuck out of this," Caleb snaps at him.

"That wedding ring says I'm not even a little fucking scared of you. It also says I don't think you'll be around long enough to matter." He leans forward. "And maybe, just maybe, my wife is a dude as big and bad as me."

Caleb just stares at him, his attention slowly sliding to me. "Your father's smarter than you seem to ever give him credit for being. He knew you'd come to me. He made sure I'd deliver the messages he planned. It's your move, man." He stands up and starts walking.

# Chapter Forty-One

## Alana

Some people might think I should call Damion over and over and beg him to come home for fear he will do something rash. But I know that man and all I will do is drive home my fear over our situation, and my fear is exactly what he wants to end. It may actually push him to do more, to act harsher.

So I resist and it's not an easy task.

I spend the first two hours Damion is gone trying to busy myself.

I organize my things, walk the apartment, search cabinets to get the lay of the land, and finally take the long bubble bath I wouldn't be able to back at my apartment and do so for me and him. It will please him to know I did something I love that I could only do because I'm now living here. When I'm thoroughly spiced up with the smell of bubbles, I dry off, and dress in a silk gown and robe. At this point, I have no choice but to cave to the grumbles of my belly. Entering the kitchen, I turn on the radio that's built into the wall. Once Luke Combs is attempting to fill my mind with his lyrics, not worry, I hunt down food. I end up sitting on a barstool at the gorgeous granite counter to eat a small bowl of Rice Krispies, which Damion apparently still loves, since he has three boxes. He used to eat them every morning back in Jersey. Well except for the mornings I made him pancakes. I limit myself to my one serving of cereal, still holding out for Damion so we can eat a real meal together, but with each passing moment, my unease scratches a little harder in my mind, and the music works against me, singing about love and breakups, and honky tonk hookups. *Damion's in a bad headspace*, I think, and his first reaction is always to walk away from me. He never stays. He never brings me into the solution. I'm just hoping it's nothing but a bad habit.

The problem is, bad habits are hard to break.

My bowl is empty, and I'm on my feet, when my cellphone rings I snatch it up anxiously from the island to find Lana's number on caller ID. I set my bowl in the sink and answer. "Do I really want to know what this is about?"

"Probably not. When you and Dierk talked downstairs in front of the building, the press snapped photos."

At this point I'm at the window and I sink down in the chair where I'd found Damion earlier and press my hand to my face. "Tell me no."

"Well, I'd say I wish I could, but it's going to deliver scorching ratings."

I open my mouth to object when she adds, "But I don't want to screw things up with you and Damion, for somewhat personal reasons. You don't think you two will be a problem for the show. I'm not convinced. I don't want him upset."

"But I don't matter?"

"You know the difference. Google the stories. They're everywhere. They'll be even broader by morning. You better warn your man."

"Right. Thank you."

We disconnect and I don't google to see the story myself. I just can't right now. I pour some of the whiskey into Damion's glass, the act of sharing, comforting in some undecipherable way. After a sip burns my throat and warms my chest, I decide I have to look at what is being said before Damion does. I down the remainder of the whiskey I've poured, and the burn has me panting. A head rush follows but I doubt I'll regret my decision considering what I'm about to do. I google my name and there I am, talking with Dierk, and the headline reads: *Dierk or Damion? Who Will Win the Heart of the Queen of Real Estate and TV Ratings?* I refill my glass and a text buzzes on my phone from Dierk of all people: *Should we tell them you turned me down?*

*Sorry*, I type in reply. *I don't know why I've become such tabloid fodder.*

*You should pay me back by letting me take you to coffee.*

I grit my teeth. *You know I'm with Damion.*

*Do I?*

*Yes*, I reply, *YOU DO*. And I absolutely use caps.

*Caps. She's angry. I'll back off, but the offer stands. Goodnight, Alana.*

*Damn skippy, I'm angry*, I think, and we're thankfully done with this exchange.

I set my phone down and curl up into the chair, pulling a blanket from the edge over me and snuggling beneath. I want to call Damion but not for the first time tonight I think of that day I'd sat at the table with him when his "friend" had insulted me. Damion had lashed out at him, gone for the jugular and he's clearly in fight mode. If he's with his father, and I call him, my name on his caller ID, reminding him that I'm here waiting, could set him off.

My lashes lower, and I decide if he's not back in the next forty-five minutes I'll reverse strategy. Okay, no. I'm weak. I can't wait another forty-five minutes. I text him: *You have no idea how much restraint I've shown not calling and texting. I need you. Please come home.* I wait for a reply and wait some more. I set the phone down, my belly in knots. I'm empty right now, so very empty, and I dare one more sip of the whiskey, drugging my mind, and yet, it still leads me to bad feelings and worse insecurities. But at least this time when my lashes lower, a laden feeling overcomes me, and I begin to drift off to sleep.

Alone.

My first night living with Damion.

# Chapter Forty-Two

## *Damion*

I don't turn to watch Caleb depart. Savage does that for me.

Instead, I lean back in my seat, and allow myself to process what just happened and replay the message at the core of this meeting; walk away and this is over. Caleb says I don't give my father credit. If either of them believe this conversation is the best way to get rid of me, I think they both don't give *me* enough credit.

It's time to get the hell out of this shitty bar.

I stand up and Savage stands with me. Neither of us speak. Both of us are smart enough to know there could be mics and cameras everywhere. This was all planned. For all we know, Caleb probably expected us to find his little girl. I doubt she's even really his daughter. He'd never be stupid enough to let us find her.

In silence we walk through the bar and when we're in the backseat of the vehicle, the door shut, then and only then does Savage say, "He's worried about his daughter which you handled like a class act and perfectly."

"I don't even know if I believe the daughter isn't a planted story."

"Blake would have known. It's not. And I know monsters like Caleb. The only part of him that's still human is the part that loves his daughter and he does."

I need to think and I can't do that with Savage shoving his opinions down my throat. The SUV starts moving. "Drop me at my office."

Savage's eyes glint with what looks to me like refusal, that he smartly reconsiders, before speaking over his shoulder to the driver, his voice muted enough that I can't hear him and I don't care anyway. I'm already on a second replay of the meeting with Caleb, analyzing all the nuances. Nearly fifteen minutes of traffic later, we arrive at the West office building.

I exit the SUV without a word to Savage, but any hope of silencing the noise in my head goes south when I find Blake Walker waiting on me.

He's a big man, talk and dark, with brown eyes who manages to be disarming and imposing I suspect to many in the same moment. Right now, all he is to me, is poorly timed.

"I need a minute, Blake," I say. "We'll talk tomorrow." I start walking.

"I'm here to help you end this," he calls out.

I halt and rotate to face him. "Assuming you heard everything tonight, or at least listened to Savage's opinions, he's wrong. Caleb isn't telling the truth. And you know how I know that?" I don't give him time to answer, adding, "Not only do I know my father will never let me walk away, so does he."

"What does that mean to you?"

"From where I stand there's only one way to end this. My father has to die. The only reason I won't do that myself is Alana and what it will do to me and her. But if that's the only option I have to protect her, I'll do it anyway. In other words, find me another answer, and it has to be now." I rotate and stride toward the door, and I don't stop until I've traveled a path through the dark offices and entered my office, where I don't bother with the lights.

The brightness of the moon and stars burn through the windows, illuminating the room and I walk to the bar as I pour a shot of the most expensive whiskey I own. After which I step to the window and think of that moment when Alana was straddling me, begging me to stay with her, and yet I'm here. Fuck me, how has this night become *this*. I should be with her, but I don't even know what that means.

There's a shift in the air and while I don't turn, I know Caleb's energy. He walks to the bar, pours a drink, and steps to my side. For long seconds that stretch to a full minute we just stand there until he says, "You know what we have to do. It's the only way out for both of us."

It feels convenient. Like a trap and I don't bite. I don't even look his direction. "You do what you have to do. I'll do what I have to do."

Seconds tick by with heavy hands punching at the silence before he downs his drink, sets the glass on the window ledge and then turns and walks away. I snatch my phone from my pocket and text Blake: *Caleb was just here, suggesting we partner up against my father. It was a trap. All of this is a trap. I'll call you in the morning. I don't want to talk about it tonight, but I do want to have a conversation.*

I send the message and only then do I notice the unread message from Alana: *You have no idea how much restraint I've shown not calling and texting. I need you. Please come home.*

I plant my hand on the window, a streak of lightning in the distance, warning me that I'm the calm before the storm. My chin lowers to my chest with the punch of emotions I feel that only Alana can stir in me. She's "home" waiting on me. It's everything I have ever wanted. But I'm beginning to think it's everything my father has ever wanted, too.

# Chapter Forty-Three

I enter the apartment to the dim glow of a living room lamp, the sound of country music, and the sweet scent of perfume scenting the air, but Alana is nowhere in sight. I shrug out of my jacket and hang it on the coatrack, and then just stand there in the entryway a moment, allowing myself to drink in how damn good it feels to come home and know she's here. After all the bullshit I've waded through this damnable night, this feeling—her presence in my life—makes the battle worth the scars.

That is, until I eye the dark bedroom, and there's a punch in my gut with the idea that she's not here at all. Adrenaline surges through me, and I'm across the room in less than a minute, standing inside the doorway and flipping on the light, only to find the bed tucked and the room empty. The realization guts me right here, where I stand. I turn and face the frame, pressing my hand over my head, chin dipping low with the impact of her leaving. Damn it, my father's been leading her mother around like a pet he plans to put down. I *had* to get a read on Caleb.

I shove off the wall. I'm going to get her. No more running from each other.

I head for the door, and there's a shift in the air—a soft whisper of a sound that halts me in my steps and draws my gaze toward the chairs. That's when Alana shifts in the one she's claimed, and I can see her there when moments before I could not. Relief floods my system with the intensity of a tsunami, and it actually takes me a minute to fully process that emotion. The idea of her being gone destroyed me. There was a time when I would have seen my reaction to her as weakness, because my father did.

Not anymore.

My father is a fool in a CEO chair he wears like a disguise of genius.

I will bleed for her. And he will, too, if that's what it takes to protect her.

I cross the room and find her curled up in the same chair I'd been sitting in earlier. I kneel in front of her, drinking in the sweet image of her in slumber. Her long, dark lashes are wispy half-moons against her pale skin, her brown hair silk against the satin of a robe I can only assume she wore for me. She is beautiful, peaceful even, when I know she was feeling anything but when she fell asleep. And as much as I want to touch her in this moment, I do just what I did all those times as a teen when she'd fall asleep next to me in my family's media room: I draw out the moment, watching her, savoring how damn beautiful she is, how perfect. But the difference between now and the past is that way back then, I'd hungered to make her mine, and now she *is* mine.

With gentle fingers, I caress her hair from her eyes. "Alana," I murmur softly.

Her lashes flutter and lift. "Damion?"

Her voice is a delicate breeze washing away the heat of a day that all but burned me straight to hell. "Yes," I say, a curve to my lips. "I hope you weren't expecting someone else."

She laughs and sits up, the pink silk of her gown tugging low, exposing the lush swell of her breasts, her nipples puckered beneath the thin material. She catches herself on the arm of the chair, and she groans. "I'm not very steady."

I glance at the bottle with the amber line that's decidedly lower than when I left and arch a brow at her. "Had a little to drink?"

"Yes," she admits, pressing her hand to her face a moment before she lays it on my arm. Her touch is gentle, but there is nothing gentle about how badly I want her right now. "But," she adds, "in my defense, it was the only way I could keep from calling you over and over again when that's exactly what I wanted to do. And I know good and well if I would have been calling you, freaking out and worried, it would have driven home your need to act against your father. You were not in the headspace to do that tonight."

She's right on all points, and she is the only person in my life who has ever really understood me, and we've been apart for damn near a decade. Love for this woman swells inside me. "There's a reason I said no one else could wear that ring and be believable. Because there was never anyone else who knew me like you, and never anyone else I'd give a ring to." Before she can react and tell me to stop talking about such things, I push to my feet and take her with me, but not for long. I sit and pull her on top of me, her legs straddling my hips and her hands pressing to my chest. "Now, where were we?" I ease the silk of her robe aside, and kiss the delicate skin of her shoulder before glancing up at her. "Do you remember?"

"Tell me what happened tonight first."

"More of the same, and that's an absolute promise."

She presses her hands to my face and she tilts my gaze to hers, searching my eyes, seeking the truth, and she's the only person I believe could find it just this easily. "You should have stayed with me." Her hands fall away and resettle on my shoulders.

"I do always seem to decide the answer is to leave you, don't I?"

"Yes, and it scares me, Damion. I can't get this invested and have you do that to me again."

"I ran to try and fix things. I didn't run away." I slide my hand up her back, fingers splaying between her shoulder blades as I mold her close. "I'm done with that. You're stuck with me now." I caress her robe down her arms and tangle her hands in the silk. "You're mine now, to do with what I please."

"I'm your willing sex slave, Damion West," she says, her voice and stare unwavering. "You don't have to hold me prisoner."

It's a bold and playful statement in a way most wouldn't expect of good-girl Alana, but we have a long history in which we'd said just about anything to each other. And this isn't as playful as it seems, anyway. It's about the many ways the past is a blade that cut us both and left us to bleed out, an ocean between us, and yet we've come together here, now, this night, the rest of this lifetime, more whole than either of us have been in a very long time.

My blood runs hot, my cock thick against the press of her sex to my zipper, and I tug her forward, her warm, soft curves settling against me. "Careful what you ask for, baby."

"I thought we were done with careful," she counters.

"Let's find out how ready you really are," I say, cupping her head and claiming her mouth, hunger in the way I kiss her, possession. She's mine. She needs to know it, and so does everyone else.

# Chapter Forty-Four

## Alana

*Let's see how ready you really are.*

Damion's barely spoken those words when he leans in close, nuzzling my neck, and I swear he inhales my scent, as if he's savoring it, the very act lifting goosebumps on my skin. "Do you know how many fantasies I have of you," he declares, his teeth scraping my shoulder, and I suck in a breath at the erotic bite, trying to process his words.

He fantasizes about me.

I fantasize about him. So many times. So many ways.

His free hand flattens on my back, his touch searing, heat radiating against my skin and through my gown. He stands and takes me with him, and immediately begins to unbutton his shirt, but when I'm anxious, eager to touch him and help him, when I would free my hands, he catches them behind me and drags me to him. "Leave it," he orders softly, his hand sliding over my breasts, and tugging down my gown, his fingers tugging roughly at the stiff peak of my nipple, pinching it to the point that I squeeze my eyes shut and gasp. And just when I think I can take no more, "Damion," I pant out, his lips and tongue are around the offended nipple, licking and soothing it.

He presses his lips to my ear. "Do you like being at my mercy?"

*Oh yes*, I think, beyond reason and my need for control in my life, I do, but there has always been this push and pull between me and Damion, challenges and games, that I cannot let go of, not just yet. Maybe not ever. It's who we are. "Am I at your mercy?"

He laughs, low and soft, a sexy rumble I feel in every part of me, and his eyes meet mine, a punch of absolute unbridled lust sparks between us. The kind of lust we never dared, but the shackles are off and the years have been the longest foreplay in human history.

"You are at my mercy," he assures me, "and we both know you like it, but it's so like you, Alana Blue, to deny it." As if proving his point, he scoops my backside, molding me to his erection and while I'm reveling in just how hard and hot he is next to me, he surprises me by giving my backside a fairly firm smack.

I gasp with the unexpected sting, the erotic invasion so unfamiliar but wickedly arousing, and already he's kissing me, and oh God, it's not just a kiss. He devours my mouth, and his tongue somehow manages to destroy me and turn me on, all the same. I'm dying with my need to touch him, aware of his rough fingers squeezing my backside, oh so aware. And when he tears his mouth from mine, I'm breathing heavy, my nipples tight balls of aching need, my sex dripping I'm so wet for him.

"I'm at your mercy, too, baby," he says, his hand stroking over my hair. "You have no idea how long I've been at your mercy."

"I somehow doubt that," I whisper, thinking back to the past, to how much I wanted him to just kiss me, but he never did.

"You're wrong, baby. So very wrong."

He releases me to work the buttons of his shirt, and this time, I do not fight the moment. The sooner he's undressed, the sooner he will touch me again, the sooner he will bury himself inside me and fuck me. And I'm not sure I have ever needed to be fucked quite as much as I do now. I want this man to love me and make love to me, but there is a dark, more primal side of him, I find exceedingly arousing.

Obviously as impatient as I am, he doesn't bother with all the buttons, giving up halfway down, and pulling it over his head. He tosses it aside, and I don't look away, finally I don't have to look away and pretend I don't desire every part of this man's body. I don't have to pretend I don't want him with everything female in me.

He catches my jaw, stares down at me and when I think he might say something, he kisses me, a long hungry stroke of his tongue, before he tears his mouth from mine, and turns me to face the window. It's right then that lightning streaks across the sky, a dramatic flame, lighting up the darkness, much like those moments in our past that ignited and then faded black. We're together now, and the world should be sunshine and light, but every second, every touch, still feels so damn impossible, as if he could be ripped away from me at any moment.

Damion tugs the silk from my wrists and then my gown is over my head, leaving me naked for his viewing, and this idea doesn't stir shyness in me as it would with another man. This is Damion, this is us, and I trust him in ways the past might demand otherwise, and yet somehow, that past is exactly why I give myself to him and do so freely. I am his. I have always been his and while there was a time when I fought that very idea, that time is not now.

As if testing these thoughts, he turns me to face him, his gaze stroking over my naked body, his gaze hooded, etched with hunger as he says, "You're so fucking beautiful. I don't know how I kept my hands off of you." He rotates me and sits me in the chair, and I don't even think about moving, not when he's sliding his pants and underwear down his legs.

A moment later, he's masculine perfection personified, his lean muscular body eye candy to any woman, his cock thick and jutted forward, heavily veined with arousal. I want to touch him to kneel in front of him and take him in my mouth, and I never had such a thought in my life but while I'm contemplating what I might do to him, he kneels in front of me, his hands on my legs.

He kisses my knees and that gentle touch of his mouth to my skin, hums through me like a song playing an erotic tune on my nerve endings. "I wonder how many times in this lifetime I can kiss every part of you?" he asks. "How many do you think?"

"Not enough," I dare, because it's the truth. Damion can never kiss me enough, there will never be a time when anything with him was too much.

His lips curve and he kisses my knees again, easing my legs apart, opening me to him, and now I feel exposed and vulnerable, but it's also sexy and arousing. He was right. I'm at his mercy and my hands are not even tied anymore. His hands run up and down my thighs, thumbs caressing an upward path until he teases me with the briefest brush of my nub. I suck in a breath, my nipples so tight it's painful, and when his mouth begins tracing a path up one of my inner thighs, his tongue darting here and there, I'm lost in sensations, my fingers digging into the arms of the chair.

Just when I think his mouth will finally be where I want him, in the most intimate part of my body, his finger slides through the slick heat there, and dips inside, there and gone, and he starts all over with the other thigh. I'm coming unglued, barely tolerating the teasing and when his finger slides inside me again, the idea that he will deny me again, is too much. I sit up and capture his face. "Damion."

"What do you want, Alana?"

"You know what I want. You made me want it."

"You want me to lick you here," he says, his finger teasing the delicate flesh.

"Yes."

"Say it. Lick my—"

"No." I shove on his shoulders, and he laughs low and deep.

"Okay, okay," he says. "I'll say it for you. Do you want to lick your pretty, pink pussy, baby?"

"Damion," I growl, all too aware that he's loving the way this heats my cheeks and embarrasses me, but also oh so aware of him pulling down barriers, and that's not a bad thing. It's just new and it feels taboo because of our history, oddly more so than anything else we've done.

He laughs again, the deep rumble vibrating through me and clenching my sex around his fingers. His eyes light with mischief. "I hope you plan to squeeze me that hard when I'm inside you."

I catch the silky strands of his hair in my fingers and not gently. "Stop teasing me."

"You want my mouth, baby, at least say please."

"You're an asshole," I complain, but I give him what he wants. "*Please.*"

He leans in and kisses me. "Good girl," he murmurs and I have no idea why those words, or perhaps his approval, turn me on, but oh how it does.

He eases down my body, gives my thigh one more little kiss, and then finally, he's where I want him, his breath a hot tease, his tongue teasing my clit, circling it, and then his mouth closes over me, hot and perfect. I gasp with the impact, sinking back against the cushion and he drags my leg over his shoulder, two of his fingers dipping inside me, and then it's just magic. He licks, strokes, suckles, and I'm already so on edge, that I tumble into orgasm way too soon.

I quake with the impact and it's like he's done this to me a million times. He knows just when to ease up, just how to bring me down. When my body collapses with the end of my release, he's climbing up my body, kissing me, a drugging salty kiss, and when it's over he says, "On my tongue is where you've belonged your entire life, baby."

I laugh. "Well not our entire life. We were kids."

"I started thinking about it around thirteen."

"No, you did not."

He stands and pulls me to my feet, his hand low on my butt, as he says, "I did. I also always loved your sweet little ass." He squeezes it and turns, sitting down and pulling me on top of him.

I straddle him, his erection between us, and our playful mood shifts, my hands settling over his erection. He covers it there and says, "This, too. My cock in your hand. You have no idea how many times I wanted this."

I don't laugh, and he doesn't either. His hand slides under my hair cupping my neck and he drags my mouth to his. "I wanted you then. I want you now. And loving you, baby, is just a part of who I am."

I can barely breathe with his words, and yet somehow, he's the only reason I *can* breathe. His mouth closes over mine, and the passion between us is sexy and delicious, but it goes from slow and luxurious, to a frenzied burn. Damion parts our lips, and lifts me, anchoring me as I wrap my palm around his cock, and slide him inside me.

The minute he's inside me, I'm panting, and he groans, pulling me down hard against him. "Oh yeah, baby," he murmurs. "You feel so fucking good."

He tangles rough fingers in my hair and tugs my mouth back to his, thrusts into me even as his tongue licks past my mouth. The frenzy doesn't stop either. We've been all about foreplay and teasing, but he's hungry for release. I can feel it and it feeds the same in me. I'm touching him, rocking against him, riding him without even the slightest reserve. And God, his hands are on my breasts, his mouth capturing my nipple, the movement of our bodies tugging against the suction in painful bliss.

Everything is about the moment, and I can't touch him enough, and I can feel the same in him. I can feel the build of another orgasm and there is no doubt he's right there with me. He pulls me hard against him, lifting his hips and the force of that connection, the way my body is angled in just the right spot, when it happens is all it takes.

I bury my face in his neck, hold on for dear life, and tremble as my body spasms around him. Damion groans with the impact, shuttering beneath me, his fingers twisting in my hair. Time stands still, but pleasure speeds past all too quickly. I barely know when it ends, but reality returns with me molded against him, his hand resting on the back of my head.

"God, baby, you rock my world," he murmurs.

It's about the best compliment a girl can have, and I use his shoulder to lift myself and stare down at him. It scares me how good we are. How right we are. How close we are to fine crystal and how easily we could shatter and break and the price would be devastating. "You rock my world, so don't leave again."

"I'll say it again. I know you think my reaction is to leave—"

"It is."

"It's not. I needed to take care of some business."

"What business?" I challenge.

He hands me a box of tissue and changes the subject. "I got these chairs for us. And I put tissue and a trashcan right there, so we can fuck all night if we want to."

"No, you didn't," I say, and despite him avoiding the topic, I laugh.

"I did. You bet I did. Clean up. And let's order food."

"You're not going to talk to me tonight, are you?"

"I'll always talk to you, Alana, but it ended up driving home what we already know. My father's a bastard and I do not want him to be a part of the rest of our evening. Trust me to know I'll tell you and it's not life shattering news. Just not now and it's my turn to say *please*."

I can't push him after that plea and I find I don't want to, either. "Since you said please."

A long time later we sit on the floor in front of the chairs finishing off a pizza, watching lightning streak across the sky. It's wicked and promises a storm that never follows. But it's coming. We both feel it.

"Let's go to bed," Damion says, after a particularly vicious streak lights the sky. "*Our* bed."

I smile inside and out with this idea and allow him to not only help me to my feet, but scoop me up and carry me to bed. Everything about the moment is perfect. A fairytale hidden inside the scary movie, and when I snuggle under the cool sheet against his warm body, I decide I might just believe in a happily ever after after all.

# Chapter Forty-Five

I wake to a splatter of raindrops on the window, and while it might be a dark and stormy day, I'm all sunshine inside. I'm actually waking up in Damion's arms, in *his bed*, which is actually *our bed*, for the first time in my life. I decide right then and there that this will be a Saturday in the running for the single most memorable day of my life. Damion's "Morning, baby," that follows this mental declaration, driving home the light in the darkness of years apart—and yes, oh yes, this is going to be a good day.

A point proven when he rolls me to my back, spreads my legs, and settles his shoulders between my wide knees. He then proceeds to lick me until I'm trembling and considering how well his fingers and mouth seem to already know my body, it does not take long. I return the favor in the shower, with him against the wall, his cock in my hand and mouth, and his hand pressing me deeper. I've never known myself to be aroused by giving a man a blowjob, but oh yes, I enjoyed turning him on, driving him wild, having him groan out my name in this deep guttural way that all but has me orgasming all over again.

When we're both finally dressed in Saturday casual which means jeans, boots, and a sweater for me and jeans, boots, and a snug tee for him, we decide to replay days of old and start the weekend with pancakes. Since Damion has none of the required supplies, we do the next best thing to cooking ourselves and order DoorDash. Soon, we're sitting at the island, side-by-side, angled toward each other, sipping coffee, and one hundred percent downright pigging out. It's hard to stop tasting, considering Damion ordered all kinds of pancakes to try and the delights include chocolate, whipped cream, cherries and the list goes on.

When we've sampled and sampled some more, and the eating begins to wind down, Damion shoves aside his empty plate, and fixes his attention on me, affection brimming from his eyes. "I've thought of our weekend pancakes often."

"You have?" I ask, warmed with the idea, but still finding it hard to believe he was gone a decade and clung to me as readily as I did him.

"You have no idea all of the things I remember about you, Alana. About *us*."

"Me too," I say, sliding my half-empty plate aside and leaning in closer to him. Both of us have elbows on the table, leaning into our palms, and close to each other. "I kind of thought I was a little crazy to hang on like I did."

His eyes glint with some emotion I cannot name. "Why did you?"

"I guess this, us, explains it, right?" I caress the dark stubble on his jaw, whiskers raspy my fingers. "But I just kept telling myself my lingering attachment to you was because I connected you to a happier period of my life. Other times I blamed you for making every other man seem less."

He laughs, this low, sexy rumble of laughter I feel in every part of me. And this very reaction I feel in this moment, is right to my point I just made to him; no other man affects me so easily and completely. They never measured up.

"I feel the same, baby," he says softly, his eyes tender, and while there has always been a hum of energy between us, I can feel the shift in us, the growing intimacy, that says we're leaning into each other, rather than pulling away. Damion's cellphone buzzes next to him where it rests on the counter and he straightens, glances at the message, his jaw ticketing with whatever he reads. He stares at his screen a moment and then punches in a reply.

He draws in a breath and sets his cell aside, his attention settling heavily on me. "We've talked about Caleb," he begins, leading into something, clearly.

Dread fills me with where this conversation is headed and my spine is officially ramrod stiff. "What about him?"

"Desperate people do desperate things, baby. We've talked about this and it's relevant now, more so than ever."

"How?" I press.

"I met with Caleb last night and he made it crystal clear that my father is in that desperate state of mind. He's going to do something that can't be undone."

Ice slides through me and I shiver inside. The obvious question would be: what? What will he do? But I already know enough to conjure plenty of dark options and not one of them are good, therefore I focus on what really matters. "How do we stop him?"

"The message Caleb delivered in that meeting to me from my father was as cut and dry as it gets. If I sell my stock and walk away, this ends. You and your family will then be safe and off my father's radar."

"Of course you don't believe that, Damion." I take one look at his guarded expression and gape at him. "Are you serious right now, Damion? You believe that? No. You don't believe this, right?" He opens his mouth to answer and I can read what comes next and I am not going to like it. I throw my hand up stop sign fashion. "Oh my God. *Damion.* Think about this. He *often* dangled a carrot in front of you, made you chase it, and then ate it himself. This will be no different. You'll hand everything over to him and then he'll use me and my family to lure you back to the company. And if that happens, you'll have no leverage. You'll become whatever he wants you to become."

He says nothing and that tells me everything. "This ends us. Why don't you see that?" I slide off the chair and throw my hands up and turn away from him.

I've made it all of two steps when he pulls me around to him. "You do know you haven't let me say one damn word, don't you?"

"You said a lot of words without opening your mouth, Damion."

He scowls and runs a hand through his hair, his hands planting on his hips. "I don't know what you want me to say to you right now. I know more than anyone my father will fuck me, Alana, but I have to buy time and find another answer."

"You're making decisions to protect me, Damion."

"Hell yes, I am, but I'm no fool Alana. You need to trust me to handle this. I wouldn't be with you right now, if I didn't plan to decisively end him."

"How?"

"I don't want you getting in the middle of this shit, any more than you already are."

"So that's how it is? You do. I behave?"

"Oh come on, Alana. I don't deserve that. I've never been that guy."

"You have that side to you, Damion. You know you do."

His energy spikes in the air. "Because I'm like my father?"

"Do not twist my words. I did not say that or suggest that. You're still the future king and we both know that requires dominance and arrogance, but I will never kneel to you. I'm not everyone else."

"You don't see what is happening right now. I'm kneeling for you, and I do it with everything I am, but I will never let you walk in the flames of the fire I'm supposed to protect you from. Never, Alana."

Emotions are officially sitting heavily in my chest with his vow to kneel for me, but there is a cloaked goodbye in that declaration, too. I can feel him one step closer to goodbye again, and it terrifies me. It also drives me to keep pushing. "I have bodyguards for a reason, Damion," I say, my voice softer now. "I think I can figure it out. You've all but told me the man has killed people and pulled you into it. I know, okay? I know. Can we get that out there right now, and be done with it?"

"You don't fucking know, Alana. People disappear when they cross him, and I made a few of the calls to Caleb to make it happen."

"So you implied. I get it. I already said I get it."

"You're doing what I did. You're pretending it doesn't really matter. You're pretending it's not what you think. *I pretended* being the messenger didn't matter, but it did." He presses his hand to his face and drops it, a bitter laugh sliding from his lips. "Ironically, it was the guy who I helped him drive to suicide that finally woke me up. He fucking did it in front of me, shot himself, and I blinked and his blood was all over me. I couldn't pretend that wasn't real. Fuck. I need to go out for a while." He turns, offering me his back, his shoulders knotted beneath his tee.

At this point, everything he's spoken in the last two minutes is exploding in my mind in mini little blasts of information, but none of it shocks me. His father is a brutal monster and Damion had already warned me this was coming. He faces me, lets me see the suffering in his eyes. "I'll be back later." He starts walking.

I'm gutted by the level of pain I see in his eyes, the soul-deep pain tearing at him and now me, but it's that very reaction that tells me he's the same man I fell in love with years ago. Who I still love now, but I'm also furious with him. He's walking away. He's leaving. Damn him. "I thought you weren't doing this again, Damion," I shout after him. "Every time you just walk away. That's what's tearing us apart. I told you I wouldn't move in with you if you were going to do this, and yet, here we are, one night in, and you're leaving again."

He whirls on me, not as far away as I'd thought, his emotions dark, and suffocating in their intensity. "What part of you're better off without me do you not get? I tried to leave you alone, Alana. I stayed away. You should have fucking married someone else."

I recoil and hug myself. "Okay. Yes. Okay." Tears prickle in my eyes and I hurt. I hurt so very badly, the way only he can hurt me.

He curses and then he's in front of me, pulling me to him, and his touch is fire, the friction between us flames. "That's not what I want," he says, his voice a gravelly, rough baritone. "It's not what I have *ever wanted,* but did you not hear what I told you? I'm not a good person, Alana. Why the hell are you not the one walking to the door?"

"Because I love you and I don't think love is logical. I also know you're not your father. You want to make things right, so do it. Make things right. And stop walking away, damn it. Just stop!" The words are all but ripped from my throat by way of my emotions.

His hands come down on my face and he tilts my gaze to his. "I'm standing right here. I'm right here, Alana."

"But you wanted to walk away."

"I didn't want to look in your eyes after I told you what I've done. I didn't want to see the rejection." He presses his forehead to mine. "I'm not the boy next door anymore."

Tension uncurls in my belly with his confession and my fingers curl on his jaw. "You are to me," I whisper.

He pulls back to stare down at me, his fingers fanning my face, and the torment I'd seen in him moments before has gone nowhere. "I don't deserve you." With this declaration, his mouth closes over mine, and I moan with the deep stroke of tongue, gone too soon as he tears his mouth from mine. "I'm not good for you."

"Those words are destructive. You know that, right? They drive us apart."

"I want to be your hero, baby, but the stakes are high. You have to know that."

My fingers ball in the soft cotton of his t-shirt. "There's a way to fix this. There's always a way."

"Not as long as he's alive. That's the cold hard truth."

"Think of something else. What was that text you got?"

"Walker wants to meet."

"Why?"

"They know we're backed in a corner," he explains. "They want to help us get out."

"So let's go talk to them."

"Not us. Me. They want to talk to me alone."

Realization hits me. "They don't think you can be objective about what to do next with me in the room."

"Look, baby, with you next to me, all I can think about is-"

"Protecting me," I supply, and this touches me, and how can it not? He's the only person in my life who's ever looked out for me. "I know,"

I add. "And that matters more than you know. Go alone. I need to go see my mother anyway. I might glean some information that helps us."

"You sure you want to do that?"

"No," I admit, "but I think we need me to do that."

He considers me a moment, his lips tight as is his tone when he finally says, "It's a good move but you have to have security with you."

"I'm not going to argue on that point. After last night, I might need someone to pry her off me."

His hands settle on my shoulders. "I'm going to take care of this and you. I promise."

"And I'll take care of you," I promise, wrapping my arms around him, pressing my head to his chest, and holding him tight.

# Chapter Forty-Six

Both Adam and Savage arrive at the same time and by the time we've exchanged greetings Savage has inhaled what's left of the pancakes. "Clean up, complete," he says, walking to the fridge and grabbing a bottle of water and lifting it Damion's direction. "Ready, man?"

Damion and I both laugh while Adam just shakes his head. "We ate breakfast," Adam says, "in case you were wondering."

"I'm a growing boy," Savage explains. "And I need energy to beat all the asses in need of beating."

*He might be right on that one*, I think.

A few minutes later, the whole lot of us are downstairs with two SUVs parked at the front of the building. Damion walks me to the backdoor of one of them and kisses me. "I won't be long. Don't you be either."

I happily agree and he opens my door, helping me inside and too soon, he's gone, and Adam's joining me. "Your mother's place?"

I glance at the time on my phone which reads ten am. "No," I say. "She always goes in on Saturdays until noon and I need to grab a few things in my office anyway."

He leans back and speaks to the driver and I glance at my phone and realize, Damion doesn't know about Dierk. Oh God. I didn't tell Damion about Dierk. I sit up. "Wait. Can you stop Damion? I need to tell him something and it's urgent."

Adam doesn't so much as blink. He leans back to the driver and says something before he snatches his cellphone and punches in a number. A moment later he says, "She needs Damion." He listens a moment. "Copy that." He disconnects. "He's still here."

I'm already reaching for the door, when it opens and Damion appears, concern etched in his strong features. "What's up, baby?"

I scoot all the way over. "Outside," I say.

He backs up and I join him on the street, shutting the door. "You need to see something." I reach for my phone and he catches my hand. "Dierk. I know. Believe me, I fucking know. Savage texted me this morning right after we got up."

"I'm sorry. I should have told you, but I was just lost in us. He was the last person on my mind. Why didn't you tell me?"

"Because I told you I could handle this shit and I wasn't going to let him fuck up our morning." He catches the lapels of my jacket and pulls me close, his voice pure demand and possessiveness. "You're mine. Not his."

"Even if you were still in Europe, I'd be yours and not his. I know you know that."

"He doesn't know, is the problem."

Guilt stabs at me over his messages. "He knows. He texted me after the story posted and asked me out again. I told him I'm with you."

His eyes burn with anger and a hint of something I cannot name. "He'd be smart to back off." He cuts his eyes and then fixes me in a turbulent stare. "You're the only person I'd willingly kill for, Alana. Don't forget that." Suddenly I'm not sure we're talking about Dierk anymore.

Before I can question him, he kisses me soundly on the lips and says, "See you soon, baby." And then he's opening the door for me to climb back in the SUV. I want to argue and push him for clarification, but Adam is already in view, and we have no privacy. I cave to the demands of the moment and climb back in the vehicle and Damion is quick to shut me inside.

Adam motions to the driver we're a go and already we're pulling away from the curb.

I'm bothered about what he just said to me and when my eyes meet Adam's I lean in closer and say, "This is what he just said to me. *You're the only person I'd willingly kill for, Alana. Don't forget that.* What is he going to do?"

"No one is killing anyone," he says. "We'll come up with another solution."

"Another solution? Are you telling me killing his father is actually an option?"

"No," he says, and that's all he says, despite me glaring at him.

I sink back into my seat and press my fingers to my temples. I need a way to end this war with his father. He has to be removed from the picture, but there has to be a way to do that doesn't include murder.

# Chapter Forty-Seven

## Damion

Blake Walker is waiting on me when I arrive at the Walker Security office, greeting me with a hand offered at the door. I shake his damn hand and say, "All formal and shit, as if we don't know each other. What's up with that?"

He laughs low and deep. "Habit, man," he says, motioning for me to follow him.

He starts walking and I follow him briefly sizing up the operation. The offices are high class, in a hot zip code, but still just as no nonsense as Blake who doesn't waste time with small talk.

We quickly land in a private room, where we sit at the far end of a rectangular conference table with Blake at the endcap and me and Savage on either side of him. "Obviously you know," Blake says, "killing him is not the right option."

I don't miss the way he doesn't say his name, ever the cautious one, this man, which I respect.

I eye Savage and say, "As I expressed to Savage last night, give me another path, and to be clear, walking away as Caleb suggested, isn't it. As Alana pointed out with accuracy this morning, because she's been around my family and my father, the minute I'm stripped of stock, and I'm out, he'll use Alana as leverage to get me back in and make me his little bitch."

"Agreed," Blake replies. "The only way you do this, and do it right, is if he chooses to walk away."

"The only way that happens is if I make him believe he's saving himself and destroying me."

"Great minds think alike is not bullshit," Savage says dryly, eyeing Blake.

"And to that point," Blake says, sliding a MacBook my direction, "here's how you do just that. "There's a million sins committed by your father in the data I've set-up for you to read through. And you need to read through it. Because you need to make sure you want to be the man cleaning it up."

"I'm not worried about cleanup," I state.

"Read the data. If you still feel the same way, I'll have a buddy at the FBI pay him a visit and make him want to get the hell out of dodge, before it's too late."

I don't even reach for the MacBook. "Too late?"

"Again," he repeats. "Read the file."

"I will, but you're making this sound too easy and easy never works with my father."

"I actually find that sometimes the right solutions are so easy, they're overlooked."

"Whatever the plan," Savage says, "I vote I taunt Caleb and let him give me a reason to kill him. The world will be a better place."

Leave it to Savage to bring the topic back to murder. "Which brings me to, what about the hitmen he's hired?"

"Why kill off the people you want to suffer in the hell you created?" Blake asks. "He'll call them off, if they even exist."

"My father doesn't bluff."

"Caleb does," Savage assures me. "He's all about the bullshit."

"And there's no communication about these supposed hits on the dark web," Blake adds, "and that feels off. I can always pick up some kind of chatter about these types of things, even if it's coded. But bottom line, nothing I'm saying will make sense to you until you read that data and it's a lot. I'll bring you coffee or whiskey. You might need the latter, more than the former."

"Nothing yet," I say, and reach for the MacBook, with a sick feeling in my gut. He thinks this is a bombshell about my father. But what I know, that he does not, is that whatever this is, my father's connected me to it already.

# Chapter Forty-Eight

## *Alana*

When we arrive at the building that houses Blue Real Estate, Adam walks me to the office door. "I'll be out of sight but close. Is the office open to the public or can you lock up?"

"I can lock up for sure. Thanks, Adam. I really, really appreciate all you are doing."

He hesitates and then says, "He's in a difficult position, Alana, and I understand his need to end it decisively."

"Surely you're not saying he should kill his father," I say, lowering my voice for his ears only.

"No one has to die," he says.

"But sometimes they do?"

"Sometimes they do, and that happens when it's one to one, you or them. As I said, I'll be close." I'm not sure if he means to me or Damion at this point, but either way, I understand what he's saying. Killing his father would be life or death for Damion, a last resort and Damion was trying to tell me he'd do anything for me. As I would for him.

"Thank you," I say softly, a small twist in my belly, at what feels like a conversation that's offered confirmation we may not get out of this in a good place.

He inclines his chin and I turn and attempt to enter the office, only to find the door locked, which is not my mother's normal way of operating. She always thinks someone will walk into the office, and she wants the business. I punch my code into the security panel and glance at Damion. "She must not be here. I may need to go to her place. I'll text you."

"I'll be ready," he says, and I enter the offices to find them dark, flipping on the light, and shutting the door behind me.

I lean on the wooden surface and consider the oddity of her absence. It feels off when in truth she could just be taking time off to makeup with my father, except of course, she'd rather be fucking Damion's father. I'm queasy with the thought I vehemently reject, and shove away. I push off the door and hurry to my office, claiming my seat behind my desk, but I don't even bother to place my purse in my drawer as I normally would. I snatch my phone from inside it and dial my mother, only to land in voicemail. I text her: *I'm at the office. Where are you?*

When she doesn't reply, I dial my father, who I haven't talked to much lately, but then I never do when he's off the deep end gambling. His phone rings twice and he shocks me by picking up. "Hey, hon."

"Hey, Dad. How are things?"

"Good," he says, and he sounds sober, not that he drinks a lot, but sometimes he drinks to fill in the gambling holes. "I'll be back in the office Monday if that's why you're calling. I took a little ski trip with a buddy."

I feel those words like a pinch. They mean he's in Vegas. "I see," I say, puzzled by his location when my mother said they fought last night, though it could have been by phone.

"Don't say it like that," he chides. "I really am skiing. I'll send you photos."

"Is Mom upset about it?"

"I wouldn't know. We haven't talked in three days. We needed a little break, but don't start freaking out, baby girl. You know I've struggled with her and the whole West affair. I still can't get my head around her blaming me for what happened between them."

Happened. Past tense. He doesn't know they're back together, or maybe never stopped seeing each other. "Yes. I know you have, which is why I need to tell you something."

"You're marrying Damion, right?"

"I—maybe. I don't know. I'm starting by moving in with him."

"I figured something like that. You're all over the tabloids. Look, I know I said a lot of shit about Damion, baby, and I'm sorry. I'm pretty fucking angry at his father, so it's easy for me to connect those dots. I know you two were always the best of friends. I was in a shitty state of mind, being shitty. I'm sorry."

I'm shocked and pleased at how he's changed his tune, as if he's thinking of my happiness not his own. He and my mother are nothing alike and maybe that's the bigger picture here. Maybe she was always more like Damion's father and the rose-colored blinders of a daughter didn't allow me to see the truth. "I know it's a little weird though, with all that's happened."

"But it shouldn't be, now, should it? It wouldn't be if his father wasn't in the mix. I've done a lot of shitty things, Alana. Separating you from a man that can take far better care of you than I ever did will not be one of them." His voice cracks. "I want to be a better man."

I latch onto this unexpected shift in him, not sure what's created it, but thankful for it. "There's a fancy rehab I found. It's like going to the Ritz. I can get you set-up to go. Maybe even next week. You can go straight there."

He shocks me and starts crying. "Will that make you love me again?"

"Oh my God, Dad. I love you. I will always love you."

"Yeah?"

"Yeah."

"I've sucked you dry. I know I have. I just can't seem to stop and I don't even understand why."

My heart is breaking with the torment in him. "That's the thing about addiction. No one ever understands why. I'll call. If you'll go. I'll call and get you in Monday."

He's silent for a few long seconds that stretch to a full minute, in which I hold my breath until finally he says. Yes, call."

My heart leaps with joy. "Okay. Give me a few and I'll make it happen."

"Sounds good. Thanks, baby girl."

We disconnect and hope is bursting inside me, hope I have not felt ever with my father. Something happened. Something shifted in him and I need to exploit the moment, for his recovery. Thirty minutes later, everything is arranged, and I call him back and set it all up. He's presently in Breckenridge, Colorado so we decide he'll drive to Denver Monday morning and catch a flight I make for him while we're on the phone. The chosen flight times should have him checking into the facility by five that night.

"Are you going to call Mom? I ask. "She could even go with you. They have family services."

"No. No, I need to do this alone." His voice is cold and hard. He really seems to be almost done with her and I wonder if she's been talking to him as she did us last night. "Maybe I deserve what she's done to me," he adds, "or maybe I don't. Maybe this therapy can help me figure that out."

"I hope so, Dad," I say, and my heart is breaking for him.

Whatever is going on with him right now, when we disconnect, I'm relieved he's seeking help.

I try my mother again both by phone and text and she, of course, doesn't reply. I'm bothered by her claim of a fight with my father that doesn't match his story at all. I believe my father, not her, and I don't understand the games she's playing.

I'm about to call Damion when my cellphone rings with Adam's number. "I'm almost ready," I answer.

"Damion's father just walked into the building. Your door is locked, right?"

My heart stutters and then races. What the heck is going on? "Yes. Yes, it is."

"I'm on my way up. Do not answer the door."

"No problem there," I say. "In no version of this life am I welcoming a moment alone with that man."

We disconnect and I gather some of my work, suddenly eager to get out of here. I'm loaded up and ready when the door opens and I grab my bag, and head Adam's direction. I make it almost to my door when Damion's father, as intimidating in casual slacks and a sweater, as he is in a suit, steps in front of me. And the only way his presence is possible, is if my mother gave him the door code. "What are you doing here?"

"Let's be clear, little girl," he says tightly, snidely, "you're pushing me. And that's not a good place for you to be right now. You're a distraction and moral compass my son does not need. Break up with him and I'll break up with your mother. We'll go our separate ways and call it done."

I'm trembling inside, but my chin lifts in defiance. "And if I don't?"

"I'll make you hurt in ways you didn't know you could hurt."

"Alana!"

At the sound of Adam's voice I realize he's inside the office and I never gave him the code, but he either watched me enter it, or Walker hacked the code. Either way, I'm damn glad he's here. West Senior smirks. "He was a little slow, don't you think?" He starts to turn but pauses to say, "Congratulations on your show's renewal." He winks and exits the room.

Adam appears almost immediately. "Are you okay?"

I sink into a visitor's chairs and breathe out. "No," I say. "I'm not okay."

*And how can I be*? I think. Damion's father just told me to leave him or else.

# Chapter Forty-Nine

Five minutes after, I'm still sitting in the chair I'd collapsed in upon West Senior's departure, but defeat has flattened me, and I've sunk lower into the cushion, that is, until the anger kicks in. My mother knew he was coming. She gave him the code. I dial her phone and leave a message. "We clearly can't work together anymore, and I don't know what that means for the show, but we need to talk about it."

Sixty seconds later, she calls me back. "What are you talking about?" she demands, no hello to be found.

"I'm done, Mom." My words are as biting as the emotions she's created in me. "You let him in here, I know you did."

"Who is he?"

"Don't play naïve. And you know what, I can't have this conversation with you right now or I might say things we'll both regret." I hang up and it's right then that Damion appears in the doorway.

I rush to him and fling my arms around him. "What just happened?" he asks urgently, his hands on my arms as he eases back to study me. "My mom gave him the code to get in so Adam thought he couldn't get to me. Bottom line, your father basically told me to leave you or else."

His eyes sharpen, his energy a sharp stab in the air. "And you said what?"

"Nothing. Adam thankfully broke us up, but your father was entertained by it all, Damion. It amused him that we felt I needed security support and I think he was trying to show us all how easily a hole can be found."

His scowl is instant and as deep as the blade that cut me when we last parted ways. "You have no idea how much I want to go confront him, but I also have a plan in place to shut him down that I worked out with Walker. We need to leave him in the dark for the next two days."

Hope flares for the second time today. "What plan?

"Let's go home and stay there for the rest of the weekend. I'll tell you all about it when we're alone."

"Okay, but it's a good plan? You feel good about it?"

"It's better than killing him," he says dryly.

I try to take comfort in these words, but it's not an easy task. Not when he's all but admitted it's this new plan or killing his father.

# Chapter Fifty

## *Damion*

THE MOMENT MY FATHER made the decision to corner Alana and threaten her, he erased the father-son connection of which I didn't even know still existed, until I felt it evaporate with that knowledge. Not even the many sins, as Blake had called my father's bad deeds, had done what my father did himself today. With a plan in place, and a good one, I'm forced to contain my reaction to his attempt to scare Alana. As much as I want to literally beat his ass, the plan dictates my action and it's therefore important that I leave him guessing about where me and Alana stand, and what happens next. Fortunately, Alana doesn't push for more details, seeming eager to get out of the Blue Real Estate offices above all else.

An hour later, we sit in the living room of what is now our apartment, eating Italian takeout, talking through a few of the details of my plan to deal with my father and how it took shape in my mind as I'd finished reviewing all the content Blake had provided.

"He's really dirty then?" she asks. "That's what Blake's file told you."

"A criminal who belongs behind bars and don't ask for details. The less you know right now, the better. You can't answer questions about what you don't know.'

"I'm not sure how I feel about that. I feel shutout."

"You are not shutout, but I am protecting you, and *not* by walking away."

She considers me a moment and fortunately doesn't push but she does ask another question. "So let me get this straight," she says, sipping her glass of red wine. "You think he'll believe he got to me if you don't confront him this weekend?"

"I know he will. He'll believe I have you locked away in my apartment, trying to convince you not to run. He'll also believe I'm rattled Monday which is what I want."

"Okay, so then what? What happens Monday?"

I set her wine on the coffee table and drag her to her back, on top of the soft rug, leaning over her. "Unless you want to go to Vegas and marry me tonight, I'm not going to tell you that. No yet. Like I said, the less you know the better."

Her expression turns incredulous, right along with her tone. "Because you think I might be asked to testify against you?"

"My father is a very bad person, Alana. Shutting him down means exposing those things, and while I wasn't involved, there will be an attempt to connect me."

"Then you don't have to marry me in Vegas tonight. I have nothing to testify about."

"What if I just want you to marry me tonight in Vegas, before all of this drives you away? You know everything about me now. *Marry me*, Alana."

Her expression is a mix of shock and happiness, her soft hand pressing to my face. "Damion," she whispers, her eyes glistening with tears. "I can't believe we're finally at this place together."

"Believe it, baby, and just say yes."

"I mean yes, of course, I'll marry you. You know that isn't even a question, but not like this. That's not how I want to remember it and enjoy it. And we can't go to Vegas. It'll make it look like we're sheltering you by offering me immunity from testifying."

My lips press together with the reality of her words. "I wish you weren't right." I catch the strand of hair over her face, and caress it away. "I love you, Alana."

"I love you, too," she whispers, capturing my hand in hers.

"I'm going to get you a new ring that isn't attached to this fake fiancée stuff you have in your mind. I'll ask you again, in a romantic way, you'll want to remember."

"What? No. No. I love this ring. And right here on the floor of a home we share together, with wine in our bellies and our glasses, is pretty darn romantic to me."

"You sure?"

"Very, very sure."

"Then it's official," I say, possessiveness for Alana burning through my blood and roughening up my voice. "You are no longer my fake fiancée."

She laughs. "No. I am no longer your fake fiancée."

# Chapter Fifty-One

With Alana the star of the weekend in my mind, and my life for that matter, we spend the remainder of two days, talking, fucking, planning our future, and repeating, Somehow in the middle of it all, I keep in contact with Blake and his team without Alana knowing and getting all worked up. Outside of my communication with Walker, an interesting part of the weekend is hearing from not one single board member. They've gone silent, and that tells me my father is up to no good, but it's nothing Walker can identify. Whatever talks are happening, and there are conversations happening behind my back, they're done carefully and off the known record. Too many of them have links to the nastiness that is my father's business. They might think they're staying on with the company, they will think that now and Monday morning, but not much longer.

By the time I wake Monday morning with Alana's naked body sprawled all over mine, I'm feeling the pulse of agitation for what is to come, and I need to fuck. I roll her over, sliding inside her, and pound away my frustration, my hand on her backside, her submission, as powerful and sweet as it gets. It's not until we're in the shower, her arms wrapped around me that she says, "I know today is the day."

"Maybe," I say, because I really want her to go to set and just focus on her day, not mine, when I know she'll be trapped on set and worried. Though I'm more than a little happy to have her stuck there, where I can keep her safe.

"You're doing that thing, you do," she says, when we exit the shower and start drying off.

"What thing?"

"When you're preparing for something big you get intense and withdraw."

I close the space between us and kiss her. "Not from you."

"I know. It's the moment. You're just highly focused on what's before you, but I think it will work out."

As do I, but not as gently as she suspects, because I know her, as well. She paints sunshine and rainbows to guide her through the storms, and sometimes, they're contagious, especially to me, but not this day.

---

It's only six am when we pull up to the studio in a Walker SUV.

Adam exits the vehicle first and Alana follows with me joining them outside last. Adam intuitively steps away, allowing us privacy, and my hands settle on Alana's waist, under her jacket. "Feel free to tell the world we're engaged. And how have you avoided questions about your ring? Or have you?"

"I took it off in the studio and probably still have to do the same. Because I promise you, they will want to cover my personal life now more than ever and Lana will have some grand scheme to announce it to viewers."

"You took it off," I say, not quite sure what to do with that.

"We were fake. I couldn't deal with that on camera."

"We were never fake, woman. And you knew it. We both knew it."

"We hadn't dealt with that together yet. I still really want to get past what's going on this week with your father before I open up that pressure the press will be for us with the show. They'll probably tease my love life for the next season."

I cup her face and lean in close. "Tell Dierk to fuck off."

She laughs a sweet, fluttery butterfly laugh. "I'll keep saying no to him. No saying fuck off to him. He's on my show and still has to film part of it."

"I make no promises on that. Hell, I'll pay to re-film the episode with someone else."

"Stop being jealous," she chides.

"No," I say, kissing her thoroughly and making damn sure she tastes just how serious I am before I say, "See you soon, baby."

"Good luck."

"It'll be fine."

"You still haven't told me what you're even up to."

"When it's over," I promise and climb back inside the SUV, while Adam ushers Alana inside the studio.

Thirty minutes later, I'm in a coffee shop sitting with Alexander, my attorney, and Special Agent Nathan Allen who's a close friend of Blake's. Nathan's tall, fit and in his late thirties, with a dark goatee, and sharp green eyes. "You understand that if Blake hands me that file, there's no turning back."

"But he gets immunity," Alexander interjects, "and you won't see the file until I get that agreement from you and deem it acceptable."

"There's already no turning back," I add "I know he's done bad things. I know I was close to some of it but I had no idea the degree of evil that man is."

"In essence," the agent adds, "I'm handing you a billion-dollar company."

"That will be beat up by all of this and need to be rebuilt."

He studies me for several long beats, his keen eyes sizing me up before he says. "Why not just wait until he kicks the bucket and just take over then?"

"I couldn't let him continue even before I knew what Blake showed me. And because now that I've backed him into a corner I believe he's going to come at the woman I love and her family."

"Because he's fucking her mother," he says crassly.

If he means to be off-putting, he's barking up the wrong tree. All he's spoken to me are the facts. "Yes," I say. "He is. And I'm worried about her safety."

"If we do this, I'm not sure a case could be made that it makes anyone safer, at least not at first."

"Why do you think I hired Blake?" I counter.

He's back to studying me, seconds ticking by before he says, "all right then. I'll get you the agreement."

"Within the hour," Alexander insists, "or we're going to get cold feet."

Agent Allen's lips quirk before he pushes to his feet and walks away.

Both me and Alexander watch him walk toward the door and only after he's exited does Alexander say, "He's going to test you and fuck with your head. You may not get that agreement before the board meeting."

"I don't think it matters. He's already plotted to have them vote against me and force us to sue them all. He has no idea that's playing right into our hands." I push to my feet and walk toward the door. It's time to turn the lion into the gazelle by outsmarting him.

---

**"And so the queen claimed her throne and soon all the kings in the universe will tremble in her presence, and fear her wrath…"**

I arrive at the office and claim my desk and my assistant, Naomi, is immediately in front of me, a cup of coffee in her hand. "I know you tell me not to wait on you, but today's a big day. You deserve a little extra care." She sets the cup in front of me. "And your mother says good luck and she wanted me to tell you to call her about Alana. She's so happy you're with her. She said she always liked her."

Naomi is slender, petite, and the cute future grandma type, with short curly hair. She doesn't remind me of my mother at all in appearance or demeanor, but she does everything in her power to remind me of my mother. "My mother thought she was beneath me."

"She's changed a lot, honey. You just don't talk to her enough to see it. Go see her. Take Alana with you. You'll both be better for it."

I pick up the coffee and sip the dark, cream laden beverage. "It's perfect. Thank you."

"The only man as high up as you that says thank you. I'm a lucky girl to get this gig."

"Get the hell out of my office, woman. I have to prep for the board meeting."

Unfazed she taps her watch. "Too late. It's in ten minutes though I know how you are. You'll make a grand entrance a tad bit after everyone else." She smiles and walks toward the door.

My cellphone rings with Alexander's number. "I haven't gotten the agreement. I don't like how they're fucking with us. Proceed accordingly."

I'd think Agent Allen didn't think the case was solid enough to move forward, but I saw the file Blake put together. It's a brick.

I chat with Alexander a few more minutes and decide I do not want to give my father time to chat up the boardroom. That would look a little too submissive to play the game I plan to play which is anything but. I exit my office and head that way. Naomi calls after me. "Too early."

I lift a hand and keep walking.

A short walk later, I enter to boardroom to find the room full, my father at the opposite end of the table from me. We stare each other down, lion to lion, and the room sparks with discomfort. Max clears his throat. "Anyone have anything to say before the vote?"

"I do," my father states, glancing around the room. "I know you all so very well. So much so that you should take comfort in voting for me."

My cellphone buzzes in my pocket on silent mode and I ignore it, as my father pins me in a stare, "Don't you agree, son?"

The statement, meant to diminish me as a player, has my lips curving. "I do not agree, old man."

His eyes flare with hot spikes of anger. "Age is experience."

My phone buzzes again, and again I ignore it as I challenge, "Age is exhaustion."

It's right then that Naomi pokes her head in. "Damion. There's an emergency situation. I need you now."

My father's eyes glow with satisfaction that tells me he knows exactly what's going open. "I can handle the vote."

I don't give two fucks what he does. I step into the hallway and Naomi shoves a phone at me. "Blake."

*Fuck*, I think. I settle the cell to my ear. "Blake."

"Alana's father was killed in a car accident this morning. She doesn't know. Someone I know saw a flag I had on his file and called me from the scene. You need to go to her."

There might as well be drums exploding in my ears. "This is no accident."

"I'm aware," he says. "We're working on proving that. A car is waiting on you downstairs. Adam said Alana is filming. He knows to keep her away from the news."

"I'm on my way down." I hand Naomi the phone, ignoring her concern as I start walking and I don't stop until I'm in the backseat of the SUV sent for me, with Savage across from me. He says nothing but I do. "If Caleb did this—"

"He did. I know he did. I'll handle him."

That's all he says and it's enough.

She just told me about rehab for her father this weekend and new hope for his future. And now this. And I did this to Alana. I pulled her into my life, I pushed my father too hard. I might as well have killed her father myself and she'll eventually get to the same point of view. I've lost her, just when I've found her.

Right now though, I need to hold her up, because she's about to crumble.

# Chapter Fifty-Two

## *Alana*

I'M SITTING BEHIND A desk that is an exact replica of my Blue office desk filming when Lana whispers to Delilah, my director, and she calls out, "Cut!"

Delilah then shouts, "Fifteen-minute break. Clear the room."

Clear the room?

My brows furrow at the direction I've never heard, but everyone certainly hustles to comply. By the time I'm standing, Delilah and Lana are exiting the room. I hurry around the desk, and intend to follow, when Damion steps inside the room, and the look on his face, the absolute dread I sense in him, has me gasping for air.

My heart twists, squeezing like a band around it. "What is it?"

He closes the space between us, folds me close against his warm, strong body and whispers in my ear. "Alana, baby, there's been an accident."

I jerk back, and now my breath just won't fill my lungs. "Tell me."

There's anguish in him that shreds me even before he says, "Your father's gone, baby."

The words don't quite sink in. I have to repeat them in my mind. *Your father's gone, baby.* My fingers stretch and then curl around his lapels and I'm trembling, tears streaming down my face. Why am I crying? My father is fine. "No," I say. "No. What does that mean? Gone? He skipped out on rehab? He didn't make his flight?"

"He's gone, baby. I'm so sorry. He's gone. There was an accident and—"

I don't hear the rest of the sentence. The room spins and there are screams in my head, my screams. Tears explode from me and my legs give out. Damion catches me and holds me to him or I'd be on the floor. *I can't*, I think. Just—*I can't.*

And yet, I do. Somehow, after completely losing it, I pull myself together, at least a little. "My mother?"

"Walker is locating her. She doesn't know."

"Take me to her."

Walker hunts her down at her apartment, and I'm the one who tells her my father is dead. Despite barely holding it together, I manage to hold her as she cries, but there is a coldness in me toward her that is wholly unfamiliar. She hurt him. She hurt him so very badly. And she can't take that back.

He's not coming back.

# Chapter Fifty-Three

The next three days are the hardest days of my life.

Neither me nor Damion talk about his father's role in a car accident that feels far from an accident at all. Damion just seems to know that I can't go there yet, just—*not yet*.

With his much-needed help, I arrange the funeral pretty much all on my own, as my mother declares she is not in a good place, and incapable of such matters. She's drugged, she also claims, but to me she comes off more removed from the process than she does grieving.

It rains the day of the funeral, a light chilly mist for the most part, that seems to last forever, when my father will not. I speak at the service, but my mother does not. Again, she's too drugged, she insists. More like too hypocritical. After crying through the eulogy I've delivered, and leaning on Damion to survive it, I'm angrier with her than ever and I just can't make it go away.

By the time we're at the cemetery, I'm out of tears, at least for a bit, and with Damion as the thread that holds me together, we stay until everyone is gone. He's standing with me, arm around me when my skin prickles and my gaze lifts and catches on a figure by the trees. A man, and he's not alone. He's with *my mothe*r. When I realize who it is, fury erupts inside me. I twist away from Damion and run toward the pair.

Before Damion even knows what's happened I'm in front of them, his father and my mother. "Are you kidding me?" I demand of my mother. "You can't even wait until after he's in the dirt?"

"This isn't what it looks like," she says, while Damion's father smirks, as if confirming the exact opposite.

That's all it takes to unleash me.

I lose it and shove my mother. She falls backward. onto the ground and begins to sob. I charge at her, ready to jump on her—I'm not in my right mind—when Damion grabs me from behind and holds onto me.

My mother is now wet and muddy and on her hands and knees. "What was that?" she screams at me. "Who are you?"

"Who are *you*?" I demand. "The last conversation I had with him he talked about you and this monster. The way you hurt him is unforgivable."

My mother shoves to her feet and sobs, rushing away, a coward who will be naked with Damion's father before the hour is up, I suspect.

"You were quite hard on her, don't you think?" West Senior dares to say.

"You killed him," I say, my voice as brittle as ancient wood. "I'm going to make you pay." I twist and jerk from Damion's grip and start walking, my pace fast but measured. and I know then me and Damion are done, and not because I don't love him. Because of what I'm going to do to his father, what I will go down for, pay for, alone, just me, not him.

I reach the limo waiting on us and Damion's there, in front of me. He doesn't have to turn me to face him. I do it myself. "We're done," I declare. "I'm done, Damion. I'm going to my apartment. I'm not going with you."

"Alana, don't do this," he pleads, torment in his eyes, in that rich timbre of his voice, I love so much, but when he reaches me, I hold up a hand.

"No. Just no. I need time. I need space. I need a lot of things I can't have with you."

He recoils as if slapped and I climb inside the car and yank the door shut. "Drive," I say, and once we're out of the cemetery I direct him to a hotel. Damion will look for me. I won't be there.

I'm on a cold, hard hotel bed despite the luxury of the room, when I dial Lana. "Are you okay?"

"I'm fine. I'll be back for the live event Saturday."

"You do not have to do this."

"Oh, I do, and I've been thinking of your need to delve into my personal life. Do that interview you wanted with me and I'll give you your ratings."

She's silent a moment. "This feels grief driven."

"It's ratings driven. I'll see you then."

My cellphone rings with Damion's number and I turn it off.

# Chapter Fifty-Four

I don't go home or take Damion's calls before the live event. He'll convince me not to move forward with my plan, but I do miss him. I miss him so very much, but our lives have been a collision course of heartache and now death.

I arrive at the auditorium where there will soon be a live audience. My hair and makeup are done by some celebrity stylist, and I barely notice what I look like. I'm nervous and numb, but I'm committed to my plan. When finally, I step on stage, I know Damion's in the audience. As crazy as it seems, I can feel him close, but I cannot let this fact detour me from my goal.

I appear on stage and the crowd goes nuts. Nerves jump around in my belly, but I wave and smile, cameras going nuts. There are two seats in the center of the stage and Lana meets me in front of them, hugging me before she says, "Alana Blue, ladies and gentlemen." Applause follows and we claim our seats.

That sensation of Damion being near expands and my gaze searches the front row, my heart punching when my eyes land on him just in front of me. Adrenaline surges and I cut my stare. "So, Alana," Lana says. "So funny, right? I'm Lana and you're Alana. Us together was meant to be, don't you think?'

I laugh a forced laugh, but I'm practiced enough I don't think anyone else knows this to be true. We begin chatting about the show, dodging my recent tragedy, but not for long. Lana just doesn't know. Her gaze slides to my hand and only then do I realize I'm fiddling with my ring, I didn't even know I was still wearing. Clearly, I'm not ready to let go of Damion.

Lana seizes this action as an invitation. "I see you're wearing a ring on the engagement finger." The crowd goes nuts.

I swallow hard.

She presses me when the noise quiets. "Is this Damion West we're talking about? Did he put a ring on that finger?"

"He did," I say. "And as you know we grew up together." I give a choppy laugh. "I declared him my future husband after a kiss in a closet when we were seven."

There are sighs and ohs from the audience.

"So please tell us," Lana says. "Is there a date set?"

"No. No, we broke up." I hold up the ring. "I forgot to take off the ring."

The audience erupts in protest and it's torture as the staff try to calm them. Damion's attention is heavy like a wrecking ball. Finally, Lana says, "What's happening? Did he do you wrong?"

"No. Damion's the best man I know. He's amazing." My voice cracks. "It's his father that's the problem."

"Oh my," Lana says. "Tell us. What did he do to cause such a rift between you and the man you clearly love?"

"I do love him, but you see, his father killed my father."

There are gasps and craziness in the crowd and I know Damion is freaking out right now and so am I inside. I did it. I really said it. It's two full minutes before Lana asks, "Why would he kill your father?"

"All I can say to that question is this. He's been sleeping with my mother for a very long time. Do with that information what you will. And on that note, I think I need to end this here. I didn't mean to say all of this. And of course, he'll sue me, but here's what I say to that. Bring it." The crowd erupts in cheers and I get up and walk off the stage.

**The end...for now**

**Burned Dynasty, the finale, is available for pre-order now!**

https://www.lisareneejones.com/wall-street-empire.html#/BurnedDynasty

## UPCOMING RELEASES

The scandalous billionaires series is available for pre-order in ebook, print (with sexy and discreet covers) and limited edition foil cover hardbacks!

https://www.lisareneejones.com/scandalous-billionaires.html#/

## EXCLUSIVE FREEBIE!

https://bookhip.com/QRJATNM

**TURN THE PAGE FOR AN EXCERPT FROM THE TYLER & BELLA TRILOGY!**

# The Tyler & Bella Trilogy

Tyler Hawk is a man with secrets and a dark past. A man who has known tragedy and betrayal. He wants for little, but what he wants is more power, a legacy that is his own, and not his father's. There are obstacles in his way, one of which is the scandal his father left behind and a will with certain demands.

Behind the scenes he is a man on edge, and only one woman sees the truth hidden beneath his strong will and dominant rule. Bella is somehow demanding and submissive, fiery and yet sweet. She can give him everything he wants, she just doesn't know it, not yet, but she will. If she'll just say yes and sign on the dotted line.

**FIND OUT MORE ABOUT THE TYLER & BELLA TRILOGY HERE:**

https://www.lisareneejones.com/tyler--bella-trilogy.html

## READ AN EXCERPT

"You're going to have to share your room with me, sweetheart," he says, and he doesn't allow me time to object or even savor that endearment, not that objection is on my mind. I'm thinking of nothing but his mouth and hands on my body and this time, mine on his.

He opens the door and enters the room, maneuvering me along with him. The door slams shut behind us, and he's already kissing me again. This time when his fingers find my hair, he gives the long strands an erotic tug and drags my gaze to his. "Control in all things, Bella. It's who I am. It's what I need, not a want."

"And as you remember," I say, my fingers curling on his chest, "I don't like what I can't control, which I guess actually means I like control, too."

"And you have it with me," he promises. "Always. All you have to say is no, and we find what feels like a yes to you. You asked if I trust you. I'm asking you now, if you trust me."

I consider the complexity of the question. Do I trust him to listen when I say no? Yes. Do I trust him not to break my heart? I'm pretty sure that's signed, sealed, and delivered, so, no. Do I trust him to make tonight all about pleasure? The kind of pleasure I'll remember long after he is married off to his future fiancée. Yes. That's a brutal yes because of where this is headed, which is nowhere but right here, right now, but one I can't walk away from, either. "Yes," I say. "I trust you."

"I don't think you do, Bella," he murmurs, and the way he uses my name—it's as if he wants me to know I'm not just sex to him. Or maybe I just want to believe that—even need to believe that—to be here with him, to be this intimate with him. Because I'm still me. I'm still not the "sex is sex" kind of girl, even if he aspires to change that in me. "But I want you to trust me so damn badly it's insane," he adds roughly, an edge of frustration in him, as if this statement somehow contradicts the control he so values.

It shakes me just how much I'm pleased that I've tormented him in some way, as if it's selfish of me. I know this, but Lord also knows I'm tormented over this marriage agreement he's obviously accepted. And if I think too hard about it, I will run. I will leave.

I don't want to leave.

I press to my toes, desperate for his mouth and body, for that oblivion he's shown me once that I crave once again.

His grip tightens gently round my hair, the act both arousing and brutal, as he denies me his mouth. "I'm going to make you trust me, Bella," he declares, and then, thank you Lord, his mouth slants over my mouth, his tongue caressing my tongue. And it's a toe-curling, deep, drugging kiss that leaves me breathless when his lips part mine. "Undress, baby," he orders. "I want to watch."

# Also By Lisa Renee Jones

**THE INSIDE OUT SERIES**

If I Were You
Being Me
Revealing Us
His Secrets*
Rebecca's Lost Journals
The Master Undone*
My Hunger*
No In Between
My Control*
I Belong to You
All of Me*

**THE SECRET LIFE OF AMY BENSEN**

Escaping Reality
Infinite Possibilities
Forsaken
Unbroken*
Damages

**CARELESS WHISPERS**

Denial
Demand

Surrender

**WHITE LIES**

Provocative
Shameless

**TALL, DARK & DEADLY / WALKER SECURITY**

Hot Secrets
Dangerous Secrets
Beneath the Secrets
Deep Under
Pulled Under
Falling Under
Savage Hunger
Savage Burn
Savage Love
Savage Ending
When He's Dirty
When He's Bad
When He's Wild
Luke's Sin
Luke's Touch
Luke's Revenge

**LILAH LOVE**

Murder Notes
Murder Girl
Love Me Dead
Love Kills
Bloody Vows
Bloody Love
Happy Death Day
The Party Is Over
The Ghost Assassin
Agent vs. Assassin

**DIRTY RICH**

Dirty Rich One Night Stand
Dirty Rich One Night Stand: Two Years Later
Dirty Rich Cinderella Story
Dirty Rich Cinderella Story: Ever After
Dirty Rich Obsession
Dirty Rich Obsession: All Mine
Dirty Rich Betrayal
Dirty Rich Betrayal: Love Me Forever
Dirty Rich Secrets

**THE FILTHY TRILOGY**

The Bastard
The Princess
The Empire

**THE NAKED TRILOGY**

One Man
One Woman
Two Together

**THE BRILLIANCE TRILOGY**

A Reckless Note
A Wicked Song
A Sinful Encore

**NECKLACE TRILOGY**

What If I Never
Because I Can
When I Say Yes

**THE TYLER & BELLA TRILOGY**

Bastard Boss
Sweet Sinner
Dirty Little Vow

**WALL STREET EMPIRE**

Protégé King
Scorned Queen
Burned Dynasty

**STANDALONE THRILLERS**

You Look Beautiful Tonight (L.R. Jones)
A Perfect Lie
The Poet
The Wedding Party (L.R. Jones)

*\*eBook only*

# About the Author

*New York Times* and *USA Today* bestselling author Lisa Renee Jones writes dark, edgy fiction including the highly acclaimed *Inside Out* series and the crime thriller *The Poet*. Suzanne Todd (producer of Alice in Wonderland and Bad Moms) on the *Inside Out* series: *Lisa has created a beautiful, complicated, and sensual world that is filled with intrigue and suspense.*

Prior to publishing, Lisa owned a multi-state staffing agency that was recognized many times by The Austin Business Journal and also praised by the Dallas Women's Magazine. In 1998 Lisa was listed as the #7 growing women-owned business in Entrepreneur Magazine. She lives in Colorado with her husband, a cat that talks too much, and a Golden Retriever who is afraid of trash bags.

Printed in Great Britain
by Amazon